SAVI
AND THE
MEMORY
KEEPER

BIJAL VACHHARAJANI

BLACK
STONE
PUBLISHING

Printed in the United States of America

ISBN 979-8-212-18174-7
Young Adult Fiction / Fantasy / General

Version 1

Blackstone Publishing
31 Mistletoe Rd.
Ashland, OR 97520

www.BlackstonePublishing.com

For the Mother Trees and fellow memory keepers

Prologue

Most people, if they ever saw a swarm of wasps, would run screaming.

But not this particular grove of teenagers. They simply stood around the ancient tree in a triangle, gazing quietly at the wasps. They listened and watched as the wasps danced. The insects moved as one, forming shapes, dispersing and regrouping to form circles, triangles, trapeziums. Just when their movements looked like a geometry lesson, the wasps began forming oceans, buildings, even highways. Their wings shimmered in the moonlight.

"They are saying Tree is dying, slowly," one of the teenagers said. Her voice was like a pebble dropping into a lake. The buzzing of the wasps rose. It should have sounded angry, but it was urgent. A deep sadness pressed down on the young people, settling heavily like a musty, scratchy blanket.

"Tree can only hold on for so long," she continued. "'No tree is a forest alone,'" Tree says. "'We take care of each other. But we cannot hold on for much longer. We are running out of time.'"

As one, the wasps paused. Then they resumed their dance.

"They also say you have ketchup on your chin, bro," she told her neighbor.

With a click and a last buzz, the swarm of wasps dove back into their tree, leaving behind a cluster of frowns.

Chapter 1

In La-La Land

You know what's worse than feeling sucky? Like really, really sucky? Like worse than take-a-black-hole-make-it-blacker-and-well-hole-ier-and-then-get-sucked-into-it sucky?

It's living in a place where everyone is deliriously happy. When I say everyone, I mean EVERYONE.

The thing is, my mom (Dhani, crumpled hair, crooked glasses, constantly cleaning) and sister (Meher, cool hair, cool skin, cool clothes with 6,233 followers on social media) had just moved to Shajarpur. I, Savitri Abhay Kumar, on the other hand, had been dragged kicking and screaming (metaphorically) to this new city.

By the way, I do that a lot. Not moving, I mean. Just kicking and screaming. In my head.

All right, all right, Delhi's air and water sucked. It

had reached properly muddy brown and foul-smelling proportions. But at least in smoggy Delhi everyone was equally gloomy. And that worked perfectly for my sucky mood. Did anyone care? *No!* Instead, we had to move to the land of pure air and water aka the land of seriously annoying people aka the real La-La Land. And no, Ryan Gosling does not live here.

The thing that annoys me most about Shajarpur is that sure, everyone loves their hometown—fond memories, excellent public transport, best people, so much history, and the food—oh, the food—blah, blah, blah . . . But there's love, and there is *luuuuurve*. In fact, it put the "Delhi–Mumbai: Which is the better city?" debate to shame. So much love, and all for one reason. It was the same reason that people who didn't live in Shajarpur (lucky folx) disliked Shajarpurians.

That reason: La-La Land has the most amazing climate. Like chocolate-ice-cream-mixed-with-salted-caramel-ice-cream-topped-with-hot-fudge-sauce-and-rainbow-sprinkles amazing. Everywhere else in the world—water scarcity, no access to good food, constant cyclones, and hurricanes, and don't even get me started on the seasons! It was either relentless summer and winter or delayed monsoons or too much rain and snow, and other climate crisis–type stuff.

But not Shajarpur.

Shajarpur has a happy climate—just right in the summer, just right in the winter, just right in the monsoon, and so *gloriously* right in the spring. No wonder Shajarpurians feel like they're Goldilocks with the just-right bowl of porridge.

The result? People constantly boasting about the weather. When we got off the flight, rumpled, tired, and grumbly (me still metaphorically kicking and screaming), a woman at the gate thrust a rose at us and beamed, "Welcome to Shajarpur, the city with the best climate in the world!" The rose was pearly fresh, as if just plucked from a Mughal garden. Then the uncle who had thrown up on the flight all over the seats stepped into the airport and flung open his arms like Shah Rukh Khan and yelled, "I am home."

Good for him. *I* wasn't home. I was 1,531.78 miles *away* from home. The home I had known for thirteen years and eleven months of my life. I really wanted to throw the jasmine plant I was carrying at him. But I didn't because, well, the plant was precious. Someone really should have given me a double chocolate chip cookie for my restraint. Right about then, something strange happened—the minute my foot touched the tarmac and we were stumbling off the ramp, I was suddenly enveloped by the smell of rain-sloshed mud and silvery green bursts of light flashed in front of my eyes. It must've been jet lag from the two-hour-fifteen-minute flight. Hah.

So here we were in Shajarpur. A city where—

Happiness was a low electricity bill. It was a matter of pride that nobody needed to own an air conditioner. Fans, sure! To be turned on in the peak of May for exactly 4.6 days. Or to drive away the occasional fly that made its way into a room.

Open cafes spilled out onto terraces and tree-lined roadsides. Gardens burst with blossoms and citizens picnicked there without hardworking *maalis* asking them to stay off the grass. There were sparkling lakes where birdwatchers would go birdwatching, frog-watchers would go frog-watching, and insect-watchers would go insect-watching.

Doctors were thankfully miserable because of their minuscule incomes—people rarely fell sick here, but bureaucrats were thrilled as they had to do little beyond basic maintenance here and there. It was a good life.

School lessons were also a little bit different from other cities. Yes, they learned about climate change, but it was like something that happened to other people, other species, and other places. After all, their climate was perfect.

The newspaper weather report section was called "The Happiness Report." *Not* kidding.

No wonder people had begun to pour in from every part of India and the world to make Shajarpur their new home. Like us.

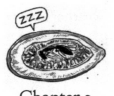

Chapter 2

Definitely Dead

"Savi! Savi! SAVIIIIII!" Mom called out. "The trucks are here! We've already begun unloading."

I kept staring outside our window, pretending not to hear. Not that not-hearing was easy, given our new house was the size of a matchbox (and not giant pack-sized). After a couple of weeks cooped up in a hotel, we had finally moved into our not-shiny, not-new-but-new house. F-203 in Builders' Building was part of an ancient block of flats, each identical to the other, each flat painted a different square on the outside—blue, peach, white, orange, and repeat—so that it felt like a Mondrian painting.

Seriously, what was this place? It was even tinier than a Barbie doll house. Apparently, it was "Dad's family home," and we were saving on rent.

There was another yell from Mom. Blinking back

tears, I hurried out and promptly tripped over a pot in the narrow corridor. I cursed under my breath.

"Oh, stop being Complain Girl, Savi," Meher said. She put one hand on her hips and inspected the line of potted plants in the corridor as I massaged my toe. "All you've done is groan and gripe about the move and the house."

How was my sister so chill about this? Why was she not being more of a teenager, like in the movies? And *how* was this a three-bedroom-hall-kitchen? It was a 2.5-bedroom-hall-kitchen at best, and I got the 0.5 room because, you know, I was the younger one. Being the younger sibling (even if it was just by a year) sucked. Especially when your sister had suddenly shot up and become tall and pretty. Even sweaty and in a crumpled T-shirt and shorts, she looked amazing.

Meher walked over to her phone, which was perched on a tripod, tapped the screen, and suddenly swept up a plant and twirled as *"Zindagi maut na ban jaye sambhalo yaaro"* burst out of her phone. She mimed to it, moving the plant closer and closer to the camera, her feet tapping away. Abruptly, she turned off the camera, shoving the plant at Mom who was wiping a moldy spot on the wall, and muttered as she typed, "New homes are like plants—they need sunshine, water, and lots of

TLC *rainbow emoji*." She turned the phone off to pronounce, "Anyhow, this one is . . . definitely dead."

Such a flair for drama that one, Dad always said. Mom began inspecting the plant closely. It was a *baingan* plant that looked extremely sorry for itself. I knew how it felt—the exact opposite of what Shajarpur felt like.

"Umm, nope." I quickly snatched the plant from Mom. Just then, the same strange feeling from the airport happened again. This time, alongside the ancient loamy smell and luminosity, a vivid image flashed through my mind—*a boy sitting in dense foliage*. He looked vaguely familiar. The plant wobbled in my hand and Meher grabbed it back.

"Savi, it *is*. It's brown and all curled up at the edges. And it's looking as miserable as Mom's rotis. Look, it's even got dollops of white stuff on it. Her rotis have dollops of brown burnt stuff on them. And both are shriveled crisps."

"Don't be mean about my rotis, Meher. They're not as bad as this plant."

"So you admit it—this plant's dead," Meher said.

"No, no, it's just sickly," I stepped in hastily. "It's all the smog that was in Delhi and that yucky-mucky water. It's not dead. The only thing dead here is . . ."

Mom winced and I wanted to kick myself. She turned

away, pretending to look at the other plants closely. I bet she wished she still had her smog mask on, so it would hide that pained expression on her face. UGH, what was wrong with me? I didn't mean to be mean, I never do, but somehow I just couldn't find a way to be not-mean.

Here we were—saddled with forty-two plants and no green-thumbed father to tend to them anymore. Or to us. Mom had always done a fantastic job caring for us, but lately, she just seemed to be in her own planet of grief and loss. We all were, really. Move over, Mr. Musk and Mr. Bezos—the Kumars had perfected the art of traveling into the void. And who could blame us? After all, we used to be a family of four. Well, four and forty-two plants. And now we were three, and what looked like forty-one plants.

"Come on, Mom," Meher said.

"Fine, you are right. There is no helping this one. Anyway, how are we supposed to squeeze forty-one—oh well, all right, forty-two—plants into this tiny apartment?" Mom looked exhausted. Her gray hair was standing up straight, framing her face like an electrically charged cloud, her glasses were smudgy and askew, and she now seemed to be leaning against the wall for support, precariously close to the cactus.

I stared at the brown spots on the plant. I couldn't

look at what was left of my family. If I did, I would start crying. "We *will* manage," I finally replied.

"This is a tiny house, Savi. Where will we keep them all?" Mom sounded a little high-pitched now.

I straightened my shoulders. "They're Dad's plants—we *cannot* dump them. Even this de . . . sickly one." I realized I was shouting. I had curled my hands into fists. My nails dug into my palms until I felt the pain numb whatever it was that was making me shout. All of a sudden, it felt like in the last few months, all Mom and I had done was to get on each other's nerves and fight.

"You don't even know how to take care of them. All three of us have such brown thumbs that we may as well be made of my terrible, burnt rotis. In fact, if someone gave an award for the 'most Lethal Plant Killers,' we would win that hands down." Mom slumped against the wall, her hands trembling while clutching a brown leaf. "I can't let these plants die, I'd rather give them to a gardener. Abhay would never forgive me."

"We can't give them away—he'd never forgive us," I shot back.

We both stared at each other. Tears shone in Mom's eyes.

It had been six months, four days, and three hours since Dad had gone for a staff meeting and never returned. He'd had a heart attack and in four minutes and twenty-five seconds, he'd been declared dead.

Just like that.

One minute laughing, smoking a cigarette, and texting on our family messaging group, and the next, dead.

And, along with it, the world as I knew it ceased to exist. Mom changed. My sister changed. I changed too.

Last year in biology class, Rangarajan Ma'am taught us about a purple frog that lived in the Western Ghats. As she had pulled up a photo of the frog on the screen, the class had burst into ewwwws. The poor *Nasikabatrachus sahyadrensis* looked like a wet, shapeless balloon carved out of rocks. At that time, I had felt bad for the poor creature which apparently was so shy, it spent most of its life underground, and scientists had failed to notice it until the early 2000s.

Since then, it felt like a bulbous purple frog was sitting on my heart all the time. Cold, hard, and clammy. Now it felt like that shapeless, heavy, bloated creature had taken permanent residence in my tiny heart-flat. It pressed down on my heart and my brain, making me feel exhausted. Constantly. Which is why every time I opened my mouth to speak, the words came out wrong. Like the steel that tore the earth apart in quarries and mines. My heart would start hammering, my mouth felt dry, and all the nice words I meant to say would just flop out of my brain. I was cold and hard to everyone.

To Mom. To Meher. To Shabana Fufi, our neighbor in Delhi. To Mamta Mausi, who had worked in our home since the day I was born. To Raghu Uncle, who had ironed our clothes. To Murthy Sir, my favorite teacher. To Khosla Ma'am, the teacher I dreaded most. To Rahul, Chetna, and Firoze, my friends in school. To everyone. Soon, it felt easier to say little or nothing. Now I'd never see them again, which meant there was no chance of saying anything mean—the one good thing about this move.

A move that Mom made voluntarily. To get away from it all. New job, new beginnings or some rubbish like that.

Shajarpur. What sort of a name was that for a metro city—even if the air was miraculously clean and the weather perfect, untouched by climate change? Where people didn't need to wear masks. How could the world keep spinning, how was everyone so happy when it felt like my heart was never going to beat again? How could it—with that purple frog squatting on it?

I really didn't know what to tell Mom. But just then Dad's pet plant (he insisted he didn't have one, but we all knew it was the jasmine) shuddered even though there was no wind. What was up with these plants, I wondered, as a sweet, sad smell enveloped us. For a moment, the cold, hard grip of steel around my heart loosened.

"I will figure out how to take care of them," I said while watching Meher as she held out her hand and helped Mom up. No one else was dying around here.

Chapter 3

The Cat in the Flat

Many intolerable hours later, the furniture had been pushed to the right corners, the beds were made up, and the kitchen was almost set up. Mom was on a mission to slot everything into its right space in record time. We weren't even sweating much in this La-La Land weather. Cartons had been deposited in each of our rooms. Paintings and photo frames had been propped up, ready to be hung on the currently bare walls. Everything had found its place, except for Dad's plants.

Munna Bhai, who had delivered the last of the plants, sorrowfully said, "Madam, Boss had told you in Delhi only, plants very hard to transport. Delicate, no? Five gone—dead. Actually, this one seems half okay." He held up a spiky plant that looked like a Christmas tree. After a nervous glance at me, Mom simply asked him to put all the plants next to the other plants that had already been unpacked. Then lots of things happened together.

A black cat ran into the apartment.

The security guard came running in behind her.

An uncle came running behind both of them.

"Shoo, shoo!" he said, striding in uninvited. He had a slight pot belly, a receding hairline, and thick glasses. The cat that he was trying to diligently shoo away had curled up in the jasmine plant pot. I almost expected her to break into a Cheshire Cat smile.

The security guard said, panting, "Sorry, madam. This Bekku, she—" But before he could continue, the uncle turned and folded his hands. "Namaste, welcome to Builders' Building. I am Mr. Kulkarni." He then turned to Meher and me and said with an oily smile, "Kulkarni Uncle. This cat used to live here. But the Patils moved to a bigger flat, and they decided it's better, you know, for this cat to continue living here. Also, they got a husky who didn't like cats so . . . I am the society secretary, I will get it out. Shoo, shoo!"

The cat didn't move. Only her tail swished.

"You!" Kulkarni Uncle snapped his fingers at the security guard and pointed at the cat. The security guard hovered by the door.

I couldn't believe it. How could people just leave family behind? What was *wrong* with the world?

Oops! I realized I had said that aloud as four pairs of eyes turned towards me. Five, if you counted Bekku. And yes, she counted.

I turned to Mom as Meher knelt down next to the cat, whose eyes were like green lanterns.

"People can be so mean, no?" Mom said. "You come visit us, as often as you like."

Bekku yawned, clearly unimpressed by this piece of information.

"What do you mean visit?" I asked. "Mom, she's staying, isn't she? She *has* to."

For once Meher agreed with me and we began to chant, "Please, please, please, please, Mom, please, please, please!"

"Looks like we've inherited a cat along with the plants," Mom said finally, a ghost of a smile flitting on her face. She had grown up with a motley crew of animals trooping in and out of her childhood home. She turned to the uncle and folded her hands before decidedly steering him towards the door. A polite "Thank you, and yes, the weather is amazing—yes, yes, really never seen weather like this," later, she shut the door firmly on him.

She turned to us. "You're both on feeding duty." And then she reached out to pet Bekku. "Abhay was allergic to cats. But he loved them so much."

***

A few more intolerable hours later, collapsed on our squishy sofa, Mom, Meher, and I eyed the pots and the cat. The cat hadn't moved, not even to eat the fish that the guard, Vinod Bhau, had brought up. She seemed comfortable among the plants and her newly adopted family.

Leaves, flowers, and vegetables in pots filled up the landing of our second-floor house. They stood like a row of soldiers from one end of the house to the other.

"Do you think they multiplied during the journey? Like little plant babies?" I wondered out loud.

"Eww, gross," Meher said.

"How are plant babies gross?"

"It's the way you said it—so gross."

"Girls, stop, please." Mom waved at us and looked at her phone, which seemed to be surgically attached to her hand these days, as if Dad would ping anytime. "You both figure where these 36.5 plants will go in this minuscule house, while I figure out our food scene. Yes?"

Some of the plants had found homes in corners and windowsills, but there was a huge number still to find their place.

"You mean forty-two," I said, fingering the rosemary's brown tips. Suddenly, I jerked my hand back—I felt like I had been scalded. An image of Dad chanting a ridiculous poem swam into my head. I was surrounded by the smell of basil and garlic and I could see him tossing pasta together, while singing—

> *This rosemary,*
> *Quite contrary.*
> *Rosemary will make you remember*
> *That one time in December*
> *When we made potatoes and pesto*
> *And it was really the besto.*

I looked at Meher, who was groaning and hauling the giant monstera to the corner of the living room. "Did you also . . . ?" My voice trailed off. The song still echoed in my ears, right alongside a furious beating of my heart.

"What? Help na, lazy bones," Meher said, peering at her left hand to check if a nail had broken.

I hastily got up and turned away from the rosemary. "Shove the rest into my room." I gently moved the cat and picked up the jasmine plant carefully and took it inside.

"Along with your books, there's going to be no space," pointed out Meher, even as she cheerfully piled the plants in my tiny room.

"It's my problem, not yours," I couldn't help but snap. It's not like she'd offered to take any in.

"Fine, fine! Here, last one. All yours." Meher deposited the aloe vera next to a photo frame and rushed out. "Mom, can we order in?"

"I want pizza," I yelled, the thought of melting cheese and crisp dough making up for this too-happy city. I was about to step outside, but I saw Mom and Meher huddled on the sofa, whispering. I knew they were talking about me, about how I had become this mean bean. Whatever.

I sat on my bed and reached over to move the jasmine plant closer to the ledge where it would get more sun, when suddenly it happened again. One moment I was touching a smooth, shiny leaf, the other, I felt like I had stepped into something like sticky syrup, and it was pulling me in. I had been resisting it all day, and now, I just didn't have the energy to fight it anymore. I simply let it take me all in.

I sank into deep, deep moss, lush green moss. I

smelled mud, rain-soaked, again. I opened my eyes and something luminous flashed by, just like it had at the airport. I blinked. I was surrounded by a faint silvery green glow and a low buzz. Once, I had tried on virtual reality AI goggles and stepped into a 3D world. This was just like that. Only it felt much too real. Of course, there were no futuristic buildings and flying cars.

A thick canopy of green leaves, crimson fruit, and peeling bark.

A movement, a shiver of the canopy. The boy, still vaguely familiar, jumped down from the lowest branch. He was about my age, maybe a little younger, his face folded into a frown, his shorts muddy from having climbed the tree, just a little too tight, like his shirt.

His frown disappeared for a second as he touched the gigantic tree's trunk.

I sat there, staring at the plant. Suddenly a chill ran through me. Right from the base of my spine, up, up, until it reached my brain. I was shaking, my teeth clattering. My body clenched, yet shaking violently. My hand scrambled for my comforter and pulled it over me. I couldn't even lie down, I just sat there. Thinking someone would come to check on me. No one did. I closed my eyes and before I knew it I was crying. What was happening to me? I couldn't understand it. All those memories. Those images. It was too much.

A warm weight wriggled onto my lap. Bekku. I couldn't move to even pet her but she seemed to *know*. She just did. She wriggled closer and enveloped me with warmth and started to purr. I forced a deep breath timed to her purring. Then another. And another. Until I stopped shaking. I don't know how long it took but at last I unclenched the comforter and touched Bekku's soft head.

"It's so strange, Bekku," I whispered. "It feels so real." And yet, it was not. It was just . . . I don't know what it was. But it was not all bad. So, maybe, just maybe, it's something. I don't know what, but a something. A magical something. In this weird city. With its all too perfect weather and perfect people. It made me feel less alone.

Bekku yowled.

"Yes, yes, just like you," I said softly. "You also make me feel less alone. I'm so glad you chose us."

Chapter 4

The Samosa School

I don't know when I slipped from that dream into deep
sleep, but I woke up all confused. I couldn't figure where
I was for a minute. It wasn't my bedroom in Delhi . . .
something was different. Where was I? I realized with a
sinking feeling that I was in Shajarpur and Dad was not.

I really didn't know how to do this—this whole *new-*
ness—new city, new people, new school. Even the *air*
was new. I stared at the ceiling, which Dad would have
easily touched if he raised his hands. I missed our home,
our real home. Here, the walls didn't have Dad's invisible
palm prints, the echo of his voice, deep and comforting. I wanted to huddle back into bed and just cry and
cry, but I could hear Mom hollering for us to get ready
for school.

I switched to staring at Dad's plants, twenty-one of

them squeezed into the room. Last night's dream came back to me in bits and pieces—a silver glow, a loud buzzing. I could feel my fingers tingling with the remnants of the dream, but I shook it off. It was the same boy who had been sitting in the canopy. Great, now my dreams were like a web series, episodic! I pushed myself off the bed and slouched to the bathroom, which was full of gray mosaic tiles, the color of oatmeal gone cold and sludgy. Yuck.

My school uniform was hanging in the bathroom, and umm, it was very brown. The tunic was dark coffee brown; the blouse, cream; and the socks and shoes, brown. Dull, duller, dullest. I quickly got ready, slopped water all over the plants in my room and the house. Bekku let out a yowl as I inadvertently poured some water on her.

"Sorry, sorry, how was I to know you'd be in the jasmine plant?" I was trying hard not to touch the plants, so I didn't realize that water had leaked out from the bottom of one of the plants, just where I had forgotten to put a plate. The brown water seeped into my canvas shoe. Lovely, just lovely. Luckily, the shoe was already a Nutella brown.

"Saviiii," Meher yelled. "The cab's here."

I dumped the mug back into the bathroom that I shared with my sister, grabbed my bag, and headed out.

As the cab carted us to school, Ma said, "I am not going to do this every day. From tomorrow, you're both walking. It's so close." She removed her glasses and began cleaning them vigorously. I wanted to remind her that we hadn't asked her to come along, but Meher nudged me with her elbow. Ouch. So instead, I rolled down the window and looked out, hugging my school bag. At least that was from home. Our real home.

Panic began to stomp in my stomach, so I took a deep breath. Whoa! It had been so long since I had inhaled fresh air that I had forgotten what it felt like. It actually hurt, like a knife scraping over a piece of charred toast.

Meher was sticking her head out of the window and taking a video to The Beatles' "Good Day Sunshine." I looked at Mom but she was definitely not flapping about. She was staring at her phone. In fact, she barely spoke to us. Like yesterday, instead of telling us what happened at work, she sent a message on our new family messaging group saying that her boss, Aneesh, had walked into the meeting and said, "Such great weather we are having today. Not too hot/too cold/too rainy." For the next five minutes, her colleagues had looked out of their large French windows and sighed over the clear blue skies and crisp air.

They were truly insufferable. Oh yes, the people of Shajarpur had it good and they knew it. I looked at the houses and the traffic. So what if they had to put up with small apartments and traffic jams—what a small sacrifice that was. More malls, more real estate, more development, more money, all welcome.

Before I could take another deep breath, we turned a corner and found ourselves on a narrow street, lined with bungalows on both sides. Lantanas in red, yellow, and pink spilled over the walls. At the end of the street was a massive brown gate shaped like a triangle. Behind the brown gate was a massive brown building. It was also shaped like a triangle—in fact, it looked like a pyramid.

"It's all so brown," Meher said, who was finally sitting straight. I scowled at my sister with her beautiful hair that always behaved, oval-shaped face, and soft black eyes. At least in this new school, I wouldn't hear, "Oh, you're Meher's sister," followed by long, pointed looks at me and then at my marks. She took after Mom, who looked the same but with an untidy bun and glasses askew.

I looked like Dad. It always annoyed me when his friends called me Bonsai. After all, he hated those poor stunted plants. But now I was pleased—both of us had slightly squarish faces, lots of freckles, and frizzy hair.

Mom pursed her lips as the cab slowed down and joined a line of cars crawling up to the school. "Vriksh School is one of the finest in the country," she said, frowning at the Audi in front of us. Our mini cab looked like a sparrow among strutting peacocks. "It was tough getting you admission here, so don't complain, okay? It's really prestigious—the local MLA's daughter goes here, as do Saawan Khan's kids." Mom had a huge crush on Saawan Khan and watched all his films first day, last show.

"Is that why you admitted us to this school?" asked Meher, winking at me. "Because of Saawan Khan? Really uncool, Mommers, sending us to a brown school."

"Shush, we're here."

The cab dropped us off between a Benz and a Hummer, and we joined the steady stream of students that poured in like a sludgy river outside a mine. A woman stood at the brown gate, hair tied into a tight bun, smiling at everyone. Most ignored her, but a couple of students smiled back, and one high-fived her.

She smiled at me, but I think I no longer knew how to make those muscles work. I just pretended I hadn't seen her. Next to me, Meher chirped, "Oh hullo!" I looked at the sludge and realized something. Although all of us were dressed in the same uniform, there was something about some of the students that made them look *rich*. I couldn't figure out what it was exactly that set them apart. Cooler backpacks, yes. Wristwatches that looked like they could pack your lunches and do your homework. Even their water bottles were awesome: the kind that marathoners drank water from after casually finishing a half-marathon. Just watching them made me feel like my uniform was creased at the wrong pleats and my shoes weren't clean enough.

I scrunched my shoulder as a cluster of "Very Cool and Hip People" passed by. They looked about my age. A tall girl with gorgeous hair tied up in a sleek side braid, luminous skin, perfect nose, and oodles of confidence was walking a little ahead of them. She turned to look at us. I froze, but of course she was nodding at Meher, while looking right through me. I felt like a dung beetle, small and ignored. She whispered to the guy walking behind her. Also tall but very plump, he had wavy hair which was carefully spiked in the front. He was twirling a handkerchief between his fingers.

He turned to look at us as well. Wait, wasn't that one of Saawan Khan's kids? Yes, he was, especially recognizable by his sneer as he walked away. The others were a blur of cool and perfume.

"How do you think Mom's affording this school?"

Meher whispered as we went into the admissions office. "It's very posh."

I was wondering the same thing. I pushed the question into a far corner of my mind, trying to ignore that horrid feeling that filled me when I thought of the world still spinning and everyone doing everyday things like talking, laughing, catching up. How did this world exist, without Dad in it? I clenched my fists again.

Mom beckoned to us urgently and said, "Ma'am wants to meet you."

We followed her into a dark corridor which led to a glass door. It read "Mrs. Pankhida." I swallowed a giggle.

Mom knocked and ushered us in. If it wasn't for the fact that the room was also triangular, I would have sworn we were inside a tree. Everything was made of wood—the floors, the paneled walls, the oak desk. The woman behind the desk was also wearing a wooden expression. Meher smiled, but I couldn't move the muscles on my face. They felt wooden too.

Mrs. Pankhida was tall. She was wearing a beige sari starched so stiffly that it would probably retain its shape if she somehow managed to climb out of it. She nodded at the chairs, and the three of us sat down. "So you are Meher, and you're Savitri? Yes?" She didn't wait for us to reply and continued, "Being part of Vriksh School is an honor. You are welcome."

Huh. I wondered if she was welcoming us or saying that we were welcome as a response to the gratitude we were expected to express.

"Fifty-four years ago, I, too, joined this school, wide-eyed and eager to fill my head with knowledge. Yes. I got that and a lot more. 'Knowledge, Inspiration, and Aspiration' is our motto. Yes. I wish for you the same, that you hold the school's head high and lofty, like the Himalayas." She waved and we were dismissed.

Outside the office, a bored-looking administrative lady handed us ID cards, also triangular, and told me, "Standard Eight? Sixth floor." She pointed at the staircase. Meher was sent to the second floor, the lucky thing.

Goodbyes were said at the ground floor, and six flights later, I had huffed my way to the Standard Eight foyer. Yup, triangle-shaped with a classroom on each side. VIII B, here I come, ready or not, I thought as I pushed opened the door.

Chapter 5

Cold Noodles, Anyone?

Fine, you also be dead. I glared at the dead rosemary as I tossed it into the composter. It was a look that would have melted polar caps if they had not already been melting. But the plant did not care. It had definitely not survived the move. Nor had the *baingan* or the chili plant or the orchid. They were all as brown as my school.

No, no. I scooted back and rescued the plant from the bin, scrunching up my nose as I brushed away onion and potato peels. I was careful not to touch the plant. I held it gingerly by the pot. I was exhausted and I needed sleep, because every time I touched one of Dad's plants, my mind started playing tricks on me. So unnecessary. Rest, I needed rest.

I put the rosemary next to the other definitely dead

plants. Eight and counting. What a disaster. Just like my day today—equally unredeemable.

The first worst thing was walking into a room with everyone staring at me. My legs felt like gloopy, lumpy cold custard. It was a scene that ranked up there with every nightmare. Every head in the classroom swiveled towards me, like sunflowers towards the sun.

Whoa, calm down, classroom. Even the desks were shaped like triangles, like wedges of cream cheese, and on each plane sat a student. Okay then, weird triangle school. My heart sank, because here was the second worst bit. The Very Cool and Hip People I had seen in the triangular lobby were in my class. Just my luck. They sat in a row at the very back of the classroom. Except for Handkerchief Boy.

"Ah, new girl. Come on in." I had been concentrating so much on the triangle and the Very Cool and Hip People that I had missed the teacher completely. He was tall (was everyone tall in Shajarpur? Was it the happy gene?) and had a pakoralike nose, thick unruly hair, and a bushy mustache to match. He looked like an extra in a Bollywood film, the kind hired to beat up the good guy.

Then came the third worst thing—he pointed at a seat right in front of his pakora nose. Thankfully, it was a corner seat. I slouched down and looked at the blackboard—"Akash Maharukh" was scrawled there. All right, Maharukh Sir.

I could feel the eyes of my new classmates on me, so I took out a notebook and my pencil box and looked at the two classmates who were stuck with me for the rest of the year. To my left sat a girl with wavy hair (that looked like it was waving to everyone), thick, black spectacles, and a broad smile. I noticed that her fingernails were caked with mud. "Hi! I am Sana," she whispered. I nodded.

To my right sat a boy. He was tall (so the majority of this city *was* tall), so tall that his long legs stretched out under the table. His hair was curled tight, like the tendrils on Dad's cucumber plant. He was all hunched and slouchy, as if he was wearing a school bag that weighed a ton. But still, he was one of those who made the brown uniform look cool, with his I-don't-care-attitude and dewy skin. What was up with the skin of all these rich people? A spider scurried across his immaculate hair. I pointed, but he didn't bother to look at me. Fine, I didn't need to look at him either. Let him get bitten by a spider. Hope it's radioactive. Wait, that would give him superpowers, so maybe not.

I was about to introduce myself to Sana when Maharukh Sir called out my name.

"So, Savitri KUMAR, yes?"

The class erupted into giggles, a noise that rose and rose until I wanted to stomp on everyone to shut up.

"Actually, I prefer *Savi*."

"It says Savitri right here," Maharukh Sir insisted, looking at the class register. "Roll number 21."

For the 1,768th time, I wondered why Dad had named me Savitri.

"I know but really, I prefer Savi," I said. From the corner of my eye, I saw Dewy Boy smirk.

"Okay, Savi," Maharukh Sir said. He turned to the class. "Welcome to another year of cramming, studying, and rote learning." The class roared with laughter. Clearly Maharukh Sir was popular. "I am your class teacher, and I have the privilege of having the other teachers complain about all of you to me. So please, keep the complaints to a minimum. Too many and you will be looking at multiple hours of detention, running circles in the volleyball court, and writing lines."

The rest of the morning was a blur as the geography teacher and biology teacher swung by to take classes.

Finally, the lunch break bell sounded. I grabbed my tiffin box, dashed out of the room, down the staircase, to the field behind the school. *Savitri*, I was fuming, really, calling me Savitri still, really . . . Savitreee . . .

TREE!

It was the same tree. I blinked. Was I dreaming again? This was the EXACT same tree that the jasmine plant had shown me. How? And what . . .

I stared at the ginormous tree in front of me. Its branches spread out like a peacock dancing in the rain—proud and magnificent, each fingerlike branch reaching out to touch the brilliant blue sky. Its trunk looked like many trees—one, two, three, four—had fused together over the centuries. Its roots rested like dragon claws on a moss-covered floor that was littered with mushrooms, lichens, dried leaves, and lots of creepy crawlies. I had never seen a tree like this one. What tree was it?

I looked around for the boy that the plant had introduced me to. There were many around, but *he* wasn't here. Suddenly, I whispered wildly, "Dad, was that *you*?"

The world spun as I looked at the dragon tree—so tall that its canopy seemed to spread across and over the school. It sheltered the samosa school, standing solid. Tall and just being there, like Dad when he stood next to me. Suddenly, for the first time since he'd died, I felt the purple frog shift a bit. It was so familiar that it made everything less strange, this new school, new city, even the newness around my family. It was so familiar that I felt a fierce kind of love.

The tree was like the Big Friendly Giant—the BFG!—to the school, and behind its canopy, as far as I could see, stretched more and more trees. Trees, everywhere, all kinds of trees. I couldn't name most of them (Dad would be so disappointed in me) except . . . was that a silk cotton tree and that one an amaltas? Who knew that there was a forest right by my school! Rose-ringed parakeets threaded in and out of the canopies, the air was thick with butterflies and, in the distance, I could hear the *tuk-tuk* of a coppersmith barbet.

A green fruit fell from the tree and rolled over to my brown shoes. It was a rather strange-looking fruit. I bent down to pick it up, but *OUCH!* A boy came running and bent down at the same time, and our heads collided. "Sorry, sorry!" he blurted as he grabbed the fruit. His left thumbnail had glittery silver nail polish on it.

I squinted at him—he was painfully thin and, of course, tall. He had squeaky straight hair and a sprinkling of acne. He sprang up as I slowly straightened and rubbed my smarting forehead. Rather, my five-head. Well, everyone has foreheads, but Dad and I had such wide foreheads, we called them five-heads. Why was I thinking about him again? I pushed that thought to the "Don't Go There" corner of my brain.

The boy was staring at me intently. Honestly, it was a

bit rude. "Sorry, you are okay, na? I just needed this." He looked at the fruit, gave me a confused smile, spun around, and ran off. Who *needs* a fruit? I then saw him join Sana and another girl at the corner of the ground. They were bent over a bed of plants, with watering cans and other gardening-type thingies lying around, stuff that Dad used to have as well, now lying in a carton somewhere. The boy was staring hard at the plants, while the other girl was staring at the tree canopy. Sana was kneeling down, mucking around the roots. That explained the muddy fingers.

I felt kind of foolish, standing there alone. But I went and sat under the tree anyway. I shivered a bit, it was noticeably cooler there. I couldn't help but wonder why Shajarpur's weather wasn't affected by climate change, but the thing about not knowing is that people get used to it. And when you get used to something good, you start taking it for granted.

I took a deep breath and opened my *dabba*. Shalini Tai had packed *thalipeeth* and pickle for lunch. But I could smell Maggi noodles. What is it about those noodles that instantly makes me not want my own food? Yes, yes, I know—processed and all but still. I looked around and saw Dewy Boy sitting on the other side of the tree, stabbing his lunch box with a fork. Ugh, why was I calling him Dewy Boy?

Cucumber Tendril Boy stuck his fork into the *dabba*, and an entire square of noodles rose with it— congealed, clumpy, and very yellow. I stifled a giggle, an extraordinarily alien feeling. He was staring intently at a caterpillar that was shimmying down the BFG tree, hanging by a single thread.

"Oi, Samar," someone yelled. A flock of the Very Cool and Hip People descended on Cucumber Tendril Boy, clutching rolls, lunch boxes, and plastic boxes sealed with delivery app tapes. "What are you doing here? Ewww, with bugs and all. Come on, let's eat in the canteen," the girl with the side braid said.

"Aah, you found me, Raina," the guy said, holding up his hands in mock surrender. "Come on."

Raina, that was her name. She looked at me, I mean *really* looked. She gave me a sweeping look from top to bottom and then turned away. The queen was clearly not admitting new bees to her precious swarm. Not that I wanted in.

"Tell me, did you see my score on *Metropolis Boom or Bust*? I totally beat Mausam," Handkerchief Boy was saying as he held out a hand to pull Cucumber Tendril Boy up.

"Oh *please*, Badal," said a plump girl with shiny brown hair artfully cut in a feathery fringe. "I'd beat you

with my eyes closed and hands tied behind my back."
I silently watched them as they swept Cucumber Tendril Boy along and vanished into the building, leaving
behind a cloud of perfume, foreign shampoos, and soaps.
And cold Maggi.

Sighing, I looked up. Outstretched branches and
shiny leaves stretched overhead like a vast, protective umbrella. Sunlight squeezed through the branches, the sky
was a dazzling blue—so blue it made my eyes water. The
tree's branches reached out to other trees, yet they didn't
quite touch each other. Canopy shyness at its finest,
giving each tree the space to grow, to reach for the sky.
The gaps filtered in the sunlight, forming deltas, channels, and rivers in the canopy air, an atlas of the world.
I leaned back against the tree trunk and closed my eyes.

Chapter 6

Waking Beauty

Finally! A reason to wake up. That was one long slumber. And really, who could blame me? The last two decades had been hard on me, on all of us. We no longer felt welcome in our own city, like people who had long been driven out of here. And how could we? When our friends and family were being forgotten, being pushed aside, and being killed.

We—the giving trees—had given so much to the city. It was our magic that controlled the climate of Shajarpur, that gave it its clear blue skies, its perfect amount of rain and sun and wind, clear water, and bountiful produce. And I? I was the heartwood of the magic.

But then it had all changed.

My weary heartwood first sank when the peepal

tree fell. My tree rings grew closer and closer as if gathering together for support. My roots dug deeper and deeper as if reaching out to the others, telling them to hold on.

But the peepal's bark, thickened by the passage of time, was sliced like ribbons by the sharp edge of a power saw. Gone, a puff of carbon, no match for steel.

The laburnum tree fell next.

As did the tamarind.

So did the neem tree.

And the gulmohar (though, to be fair, they do tend to fall a lot).

The mangroves, they of half-land, half-water, were the last straw, as they, too, began to be reclaimed into all land and concrete. What a strange word humans used for this—reclamation—when they were claiming something that wasn't theirs to take. That which belonged to the mudskippers, the corals, the crabs, the lapwings. They reclaimed it as theirs anyway.

With that, the climate slowly began to change because my magic weakened, as our tribe diminished. Not that anyone noticed, after all it's just the weather.

Meanwhile, in the void left by the fallen trees—grew a forest, anew.

Canopies of glass.

Roots of cement.

Barks of steel.

A not-a-forest forest of concrete.

And the humans? With every new generation, they seemed to have forgotten that they were a part of a world that was not just about them. With every passing year, Shajarpurians began preferring buildings over us trees, malls over beaches, and parking lots over mangroves. For them, house plants, terrace gardens, and crows-kites-pigeons were wild enough, thank you very much. Where local trees once stood, lantana creeps and crawls and slowly strangles . . . (shudder). Where once flew crested serpent eagles, there were now black kites and rock pigeons.

The more they forgot, the less they cared. The less they cared, the more they forgot. As they forgot, my magic weakened. Grief-stricken, I had no choice but to withdraw into myself. To try to forget, like we had been forgotten.

But now, just like spring, hope blossomed. If I could sing a song, I would burst into a chart-topping Bollywood one with flowery lyrics (if anyone's allowed that, it is a tree) about a much-awaited arrival. Admirably, grand old me showed great restraint.

Instead, I burst into fruit, or rather, with fruit.

Lots of them—not just the stray one or two necessary to keep me alive. Birds took up the chorus on my behest, as did the cicadas, even though it was morning.

Now little green bulbs played peek-a-boo in my canopy, hiding invisible flowers within them. Renewed strength coursed through my roots. It was time to shed my tiredness and gather myself. Across the city, trees, plants, and shrubs burst into bloom, and purples, yellows, and reds dotted the skyline.

"About time," a wasp buzzed gently.

The school bell rang, and I was jolted awake as something buzzed right by my ear. I must have fallen asleep under the tree! That, too, on my first day of school. What a doofus. The smell of wet soil and leaves was thick around me, luminous pinpricks swam in front of my eyes. I blinked. I had dreamed that the grand old Tree had woken from a long slumber, as if someone had moved a mouse, making their computer screen light up, and begun to complain about the state of the world.

It was a dream, right? It had to be. After all, I could not be in a weird-weather place and not have weird things happen to me. That would be even more weird. But still, talking plants and now talking trees had to be a first, even for me. Nope, I was not going there. It was all that exhaustion, of everything, and these were all just daydreams. Talking tree, it seems!

I took a ragged, deep breath. The sounds of a volleyball being tossed around and the chatter of my schoolmates came into sharp focus, along with an orchestra of birds and cicadas.

I quickly looked around and then peered at my hands and legs. Phew, no one had doodled anything or smeared toothpaste on them. The one good thing about being invisible is that no one notices you. I sighed with relief and packed up my tiffin. I should have been thinking about the next class, but try as I might, I could not shake off the whispers from my dream.

Chapter 7

The Champion of Breakfasts

Meher grinned at Mom and me over her plate of *poha*. "This is why we live here now," she proclaimed. "Great weather . . ."

Really? The weather had been fine when we moved two months ago. But somehow the fresh air had started to feel stale and then faintly metallic. Everything smelled of smog and pollution. Everyone else seemed to be blissfully unaware of it, maybe because when you have something good, you end up taking it for granted? Or maybe it was just my overactive imagination. First talking plants, now weird weather.

"And *poha*!" Meher was still babbling away. "The champion of breakfasts. I mean, they're not a patch on Dad's scrambled eggs, of course, but still. It's not bad: a cat by my feet and *poha* on my plate." Immediately, she got up to take a photo, artfully arranging the plate so that it was just visible in the frame along with Bekku, and posted it online.

"Dad actually made amazing *poha*," I said, taking a spoonful and closing my eyes.

"How did you know that?" Mom stared hard at me.

Yikes! I gripped the table. I wanted to answer, but what would I say? How could I tell her that this morning while watering the plants, the curry leaf plant (one of the few plants that was actually doing okay-ish) decided to show me a vision of Dad making *poha*? *A very young Abhay, before he became Dad, mixing the* poha, *squeezing fresh* nimbu *over it, tasting it for salt.* How in the name of monstera did it know? What was happening to me? First, the world as I had known it had turned upside down, and then in that topsy-turvy world, this weirdness. The plants, they were drawing me into worlds, some of them familiar, but not always. So many were new. I was seeing glimpses of Dad as a teenager, as a boy. I didn't know these stories. Then how was I seeing them?

None of my science classes on plant communication had prepared me for this. A joke, yes. Music, yes. Plants respond to that. But how in the world were these plants giving me Dad-memories? And that talking Tree! I felt as if I had breathed in a mouthful of Shajarpur's slightly metallic air—headachey, with a constant churning in my stomach.

But at least Mom was finally talking. So far, the only thing she had served us, alongside our meals, had been silence with an occasional staccato "Pass the aloo," or "No, thanks, I don't want the *lauki*," or "I don't know why you won't eat *lauki*—it's good for you." She barely uttered a word to us except "Pack your bags," or "Stow your shoes away," or "Did you do your homework?" or "Did you feed the cat?" She would leave early for work, handing over the kitchen to Shalini Tai (silver lining), and come back late, and eat her dinner at her laptop.

On weekends, she cleaned non-stop, putting Monica of *Friends* to shame. I would put down my half-empty glass (note: worldview) and before I knew it, she'd have swooped it up and carefully arranged it in the kitchen sink. Meher would leave smudge marks on a glass while shooting a reel, and Mom would be shoving her out of the way to quickly wipe it down with a damp newspaper. Neither of us felt like she could hold up a conversation without flicking at us with a duster.

It left no time or space for me to talk to her about . . . this strange thing that was happening to me. Anyway, I couldn't talk to Mom. The last time I had complained, she had snapped and said how lucky we were to be in amazing Shajarpur. For instance, Mom's colleague Sheila refused most assignments because when she traveled elsewhere, she hated it. She kept turning down promotions because as long as she could be home in Shajarpur, she was happy—a fact that her sister, who lived abroad, did not appreciate, but what could she do? Especially when Sheila had made it clear that she didn't have the clothes for too hot/too cold/too rainy weather. Sheila's wardrobe was for just-right weather.

Aamir Chacha, who had persuaded Mom to move (thanks for nothing, Dad's childhood friend), didn't even spare his own Ammi. He kept telling her to move to Shajarpur with him, but she wouldn't listen. He hated the cramped apartments, the traffic jam that had started becoming normal, and his hole of an office. He really, really missed Srinagar, but he loved being able to go for a run every morning—and his lungs appreciated it too.

So, I stopped complaining. And mostly stopped talking, just like Mom. But today was a long weekend, and she had finally uttered a whole non-chore-related question.

"Whaaaa," Meher raised an eyebrow. "How come he never made it for us?"

"You know how fussy he was," Mom said finally. "'This doesn't taste like home, that isn't made like we made it back then.' But before we moved to Delhi, we lived here. He, in fact, grew up in this very house." She looked around her with blank eyes.

WAIT! A bubble of excitement began to form inside me. That meant it *was* him visiting Tree at Samosa School. I hadn't been sure so far, but now I knew! Even Meher looked properly interested, abandoning her phone for a change.

I had so many questions, but Mom was still talking. "And Sunday breakfasts were always *poha*. We'd wake up late, potter around in the kitchen, I'd chop everything, he'd stir. Two cups of *adrak* chai, and that was our Sunday morning." Mom looked like she was in another world.

Meher and I exchanged glances. Mom cooked! Okay, she sliced and diced, but still. Wow!

"I want to learn," Meher said. "His recipe. Will you teach me? We can make a reel . . . ooh, to 'The Lemon Song!'"

"We'll see," said Mom, reaching for a glass and staring at it. "This needs washing," she said to herself and got up.

"Right, it's not like you could cook it anyway," I pointed out to Meher. "How would you dice potatoes with your nails?"

Meher rolled her eyes at me. "Ever heard of a food

processor? But madam, at least this *poha* has Dad's curry leaf. Well done! *Achchha*, tell me, how are Saawan Khan's kids? Isn't one of them in your class? I saw him the other day in the canteen. Mom, did you know that . . ."

But Mom was no longer listening, she was busy clearing up the breakfast table. I looked at Meher, who was already staring at her phone, smiling at whoever had been messaging her. Invisible is how I felt.

On Sunday mornings, I used to be the one to wake up with Dad, and we'd whip up scrambled eggs with cheddar cheese and butter to go with heaps of sourdough toast and fry hash browns. Or make buckwheat pancakes with honey and pats of butter. Or thick slabs of French toast slathered with hazelnut chocolate spread that we'd have just made in our mixer-grinder, whipping the mixture until the grinder became so hot that we had to give it a break from all the churning. Mom and Meher would only wake up when breakfast was ready. It was my ritual with Dad—just ours—a time to share how my week was with him, complaining when Chetna had got better marks than me in English, or giggling over how the two of us had pranked Firoze.

But he'd never told me about making *poha* with Mom on any of those mornings. Actually, I had never asked him anything about his growing-up years, the tree, school, college, anything. I had never thought that there wouldn't be another Sunday.

I wanted to fling my bowl at Mom or Meher just so they'd look at me. Only, I suspected Meher would just ask me to throw it again and insist on filming it. So I slunk away from the table and went into my room, closing the door behind me. But Bekku slipped in like a dark night. Must have been to escape a bath or something. Mom had been making threatening noises about that.

I looked at the curry leaf plant by my cluttered windowsill and reached out to touch it, but then I changed my mind. Instead, I decided to squish Bekku, who yowled in protest.

"How did you know?" I whispered to the plant.

The plant shuddered and a sigh escaped me. "Maybe Dad planted you because it made him think of home?" Great, now I was talking to a plant. And it was talking back to me. All of them were—plants, tree, you name it.

This was totally whack. Whack, but also kinda cool. Weird superpower in weird weather city.

I needed to test this again. I touched the curry leaf plant, and it sucked me up like coconut water through a bamboo straw, tossing me into sticky memories. I once again sank into deep, deep moss, my nose tickled at the scent of wet mud, and I squinted as pinpricks of light appeared before me. Oddly enough, I wasn't scared, it felt like slipping into Dad's sweater on a cold winter evening, comforting and cozy. (I couldn't help but smile at that thought of Dad and his favorite sweater, gray, and all pilling.)

Especially because at the other end was Dad.

He looked perplexed, as Meher demanded her own phone. "But I want to make reels!" she was saying. "All my friends are influencers!"

"They are influencing whom?" Dad looked at Mom, who shrugged. "Teachers? For better marks? That's totally not right, you know."

"Nooooo, on social media. How do you not know anything?"

Dad's face fell, he hated feeling obsolete.

I could almost reach out and touch him, I was that close, but I was not really there—rather, he was not really here. I blinked and I was back in my room.

I flopped down on my bed, heart hammering as Dad's bemused voice still rang in my ears. I couldn't make sense of anything, it was almost as if—

No, that's ridiculous. This was my grief causing me to imagine strange things. I wondered if I should tell Meher, but she'd either laugh at me or show me some social media *gyaan* on grief or insist I see a therapist. Or maybe she wouldn't even listen. Mom had enough on her plate. Anyway, what was I going to say? "Hey family, did you know, these plants and this one tree keep telling me all kinds of stuff?"

I knew what they would say—this was my mind playing tricks on me to help me remember Dad, to keep his memory alive. It was either that or, well, I was so bored in La-La Land that I kept falling asleep, even while standing, and compensated by dreaming up all sorts of strange stuff.

Yup. That's what it must be.

Also, I didn't really mind. Living in Dad's childhood home made the walls feel more familiar, and the memories made it feel like he was right here.

Just then Bekku curled up by my elbow. It was oddly comforting and made it feel less strange to be talking to a plant. Because Bekku was totally not judging me.

Chapter 8

It's So Unfair

Mrs. Pankhida's voice was booming over the intercom, but I wasn't exactly listening. I had bigger things to worry about. Talking plants, for instance. Like the aloe vera which had just this morning stabbed me with a memory. *A very prickly Dad was pacing up and down the hall, yelling at someone on the phone, his face livid. "But she's eligible for the scholarship," he was saying, his voice hoarse from all the shouting.* Dad had always had a short temper. He always felt, "There is so much wrong in the world, it's up to us to help make it just a little bit right."

This memory sharing was now happening so regularly that it had become like brushing teeth. You know how you feel after binge-watching *The Good Doctor* for eight hours straight, your head stuffed with all those episodes? My head felt like that—all the time! I had just gotten used to the fact that every time I touched a plant, it told me stuff. Not just memories of Dad, but also of Shajarpur, of farmers, of workers, of wasps.

I noticed Samar and Sana exchanging looks over my head as two men trooped into the classroom, bearing an air conditioner. A woman followed them, lugging a toolbox and barking instructions. The unthinkable was happening. Air conditioners and coolers were going up all over Shajarpur. Aha! I was right, the weather *was* turning weird. In fact, this town only was weird. It wasn't me—it was Shajarpur. Sana scribbled a note and passed it to Samar. Annoying humans. It's not like I cared what they had to say to each other. Samar opened the note and frowned.

I tuned into Mrs Pankhida's voice. "I have *never*, ever had to get an AC installed in my house. My family has lived in Shajarpur for years." She then went on and on about Shajarpur's heyday. I can bet that the AC-fitting crew were rolling their eyes, thinking at least these people could afford an AC and the bills that came with it.

Murphy's law, aka climate crisis, had finally seeped into Shajarpur. Worse, the people had been so happy and proud of their perfect climate that they had failed to notice that slowly, but surely, it was changing. Some people now remembered that it had begun with a few extra days of summer, a few extra days of winter, an almost absence of spring, and a few extra weeks of rain. All this had gone unnoticed. The weather reporters would have pointed it out, but there were no weather reporters in the city. They had all packed their bags and moved to places where there was something to report. The temperature began rising—from an even 68-70 degrees Fahrenheit, it was suddenly 80, then 85, and now the weather apps were showing 90! *GASP*. 90! In fair-weather Shajarpur?

The bell went, and I slipped away to say bye to Tree before heading home. Visiting Tree was rapidly becoming the highlight of my day. As I smiled at Tree, a bulbul came and sat on a branch and began chirping away. I wished I could chirp back to him. At least I could talk to Tree. Being around Tree didn't stop the hurt, but it made it a little less hard.

"Hi there," I whispered, and touched the trunk—

The soil shifted, tunneled by hundreds of squirmy earthworms. A whisper in the wind . . .

They forget.
Every generation,
Bit by bit,
Forgets—

The scampering of the squirrels,
The whoosh of the serpent eagle's wing,
The crunch of autumn leaves beneath their feet,
The fragrance of raat ki rani,
A vanishing
Of species
Of the climate
Of memories
Until the weather begins to turn.

Each time a group complained—those green, eco, citizen friends of trees—saplings were planted, and photos taken alongside tons of back-slapping. The people of Shajarpur began to forget about the outside, green world.

They would go to protest sites and suddenly get lost in their phones and their voices would trail away.

They'd click on a signature petition and get distracted by a social media post or an ad about the latest shoes instead.

They would switch on the TV, and the current coolest show would come on, and they would forget why they'd wanted to save the trees in the first place.

They would open the newspaper and a ping on their phones would distract them from any news about trees being chopped or mangroves being reclaimed for land.

Every time one of us was cut down, the natural world would reclaim the land. We would grow back, slowly but surely. But this time around, we didn't. The trees didn't return; they didn't want to grow back. They refused to.

You don't want us? Fine, we don't need you either. This is goodbye. Ciao! Aavjo!

Seed pods, that way.

Wasps, off we go.

Bees, bats, we know where we're not welcome. Don't we? We will take our pollination elsewhere.

I opened my eyes and scowled at Tree. Really? REALLY? Why were they telling me all this? What was I supposed to do with this information! This was TMI. No, it was actually TMTI—Too Much Terrible Information.

With a last scowl at Tree, I headed home. I turned the corner to our block only to see Kulkarni Uncle standing with a group of other uncles. Great.

He beamed, "How are the plants doing, Savitri?" I shrugged and scurried away. Why did he keep asking me that?

I squinted up at the Mondrianlike balconies in Builders' Building. They were dotted with ACs as well now.

As I passed A Block, I could hear our neighbor Reva's parents shouting at her for failing some piano exam. "But it's too hot to play," she shouted back. I couldn't help but secretly agree even as I winced at her whinging tone. From the jingly shiny people that they had been, Shajarpurians had become whiny people. Sad people. I thought everyone being miserable would suit me perfectly, but it turned out, I was wrong.

I take it all back. Happy Shajarpur was way preferable to whiny Shajarpur. Now, Shajarpurians kept declaring how the turn in the weather was so very unfair. If I had a rupee for every time someone began a conversation with "in our times," I would now be as rich as Raina. I could use that money to hire a gardener for my plants, who were hating this change even more. They were wilting right before my eyes, no matter how much I tried. The line of definitely dead plants was increasing and the rows of definitely alive plants dwindling, like a horrendous question in a maths exam with the most dreadful of calculations.

Honestly, I didn't get it. This talking to plants— rather, being talked to by plants should actually result in healthy plants. That's common sense, after all. But no, nothing helped them. I had tried everything— yucky-smelling chemicals, telling them lame jokes, and even playing music. The plants just kept getting browner and shoving more memories down my mind's crowded lanes. Like they were also missing Dad and his green thumb.

I reached home to see a dust storm gathering in the horizon, which was becoming a weekly thing and I knew what that meant. So far, Mom had been bringing her A game to cleaning, but now she was knocking it out of the park. Windows were constantly being shut, surfaces being wiped down, and all of us told to clean up the moment we got home.

I suddenly felt like the weather: tired. Did weather ever get tired of going through it all? What had been the point of moving? Thanks, La-La Land. Thanks for nothing.

I hid in my room, pretending to read *Plantopedia*. Since Dad had gone, I just hadn't been able to read— not a word—and that was awful because reading was my thing. Everyone had a thing. Mom had her movie trivia. Meher had her charm, moves, and now 7,655 followers. Dad had his plants. I had books.

All right, I was going to get through this book, come rain or hail. It would tell me how to keep his delicate leafy darlings alive. I opened the book and found the jasmine flower I'd pressed years ago. I looked up sadly at its plant parent, wilted completely, a sorry shade of brown—just like our school uniform. But I couldn't throw away Dad's favorite plant.

I touched the pressed flower gently and braced myself, the mossy smell and luminous plants cleared to form an image of Dad gardening in our Delhi home.

He was listening to his favorite Nina Simone song, "Who Knows Where the Time Goes." "Greatest singer ever, Savi," he said, his smile brighter than the pearly white jasmines.

The song faded away as the flower slipped out of my hand. I was back in my miniature room in a house where Nina Simone was no longer played. Instead, the TV news kept blaring about some new infrastructure projects, or a tree clearance plan, or whatever web series everyone was watching on their gadgets in their room. This had to stop! I pinched myself. *Ouch.* Terrible idea.

I flipped through the pages of my book instead— *brinjal is a fruit.* I wondered if a baba ghanoush dip then would count as a fruit salad. Who knew!

Chapter 9

Enter the Ents

"I know, you need water—a lot of water. I forgot, okay?
School is hard. But don't give me a hard time. You don't
know what you're talking about. I really have no business talking to you. Especially since you also decided to
shrivel up and die. I know the weather's awful, but you
didn't need to *die*."

I realized I was crying as I snapped the dry lemongrass blade in half. The smell enveloped me and pushed
me into the now-familiar loamy, luminous space into
a time when Dad used to make his special Thai curry.
With roasted bell peppers, lime leaves, and mushrooms.
ARGH, even dead this plant was forcing memories into
my head.

Okay, fine. I didn't actually mind it. This is what I
had now. These memories. I somehow didn't want to

share them with anyone yet. Maybe I needed help, like talking to a therapist again? That Delhi grief counselor had been so helpful, though she did say that I take everything in so much that I then lash out. Oh well. But the plants, they kept me anchored to Dad, so no, I wasn't telling Mom or Meher yet. Anyway, it's not like anyone had built interstellar gateways for us to communicate from our very different grief planets. I crumbled the lemongrass stalk into the wet bin and pushed thoughts of Dad, Thai curry, and jasmine rice into a corner of my brain. Let the memories become mulch.

It was time for another day of Samosa-UGH-School. I slipped on my sweater because now it was really cold. I really could not complain.

The cold was worse for all the people selling magazines and peanuts on the road. Everything became freezing and they couldn't stand outside for long. All the car people had their windows up, and the heaters on in their cars, and they were reading magazines on their phones. So what then was the point of selling them the magazines? They ripped up the magazines and built a bonfire and roasted peanuts on top of that.

It was so unfair, B Block's Felita Miss declared as she had to wake up at 6 a.m. to catch the school bus. Vinod Bhau was layered in multiple sweaters and a monkey cap even as a fight on chat raged in the building about buying him a heater. "Where is the budget?" Das Uncle growled and sent a "Good Night" message right after. Thankfully, the women's messaging group had pooled money to buy him one.

Newspaper reports had finally started talking about this change in weather, while news channels began interviewing for weather reporters, a position they had never needed before. The companies in the city stayed conveniently quiet. They blamed the government, God, Martians, forgetting that they, too, were part of climate crisis causes. At election rallies, politicians held events in which they planted saplings. They didn't talk about how many of those saplings became trees. Or that they had just signed a contract to clear old forests.

Mom, in between a marathon clean-up session, told us that the municipality workers outside our building— Shanta, Jeev, and Mukund—wanted to take a day off because it was so cold, but they didn't want their pay to be docked. So, they went in with six layers of clothing, which made their work doubly hard—actually six times as hard, not that anyone seemed to care.

Just as everyone got used to the cold and learned to knit sweaters, it started raining. So then we all had to carry backpacks which accommodated sweaters for the cold, hankies for mopping sweat, and umbrellas so that the weather would not catch us by surprise. Except for the Very Cool and Hip People and others from their species because they had weather-controlled cars to ferry them everywhere, of course.

This temperamental weather, I had thought, would suit my mercurial, cold, damp-squib mood swings. But no. I realized I missed Shajarpur's gorgeous climate. It had been the one steady thing in my rollercoaster life, and now even that had changed. And over the last month, it kept getting worse—like it was depressed. As if the climate had worked too hard and now could not get out of bed, just like me on most mornings. And everyone knows that depression in weather causes cyclonic activity. Just like the one that was going to hit me next.

"So sorry, Savitri," said Maharukh Sir, who didn't look very sorry, "but the Library Lions Lair is full."

I had put my name down for the book club. How can a club be full? Plus he was still calling me *Savitri*.

"But sir . . ."

"The only space we now have is in the Eco Ents," he continued as if he hadn't been interrupted at all. "It's either that or the Wizardly Chess Club."

"Eco Ants? You want me to be part of an ant club?"

"It's Ents, Savitri, from *The Lord of the Rings*.

Seriously, you're sure you wanted to be in the book club?" Of course I knew that, I just didn't hear Sir. UGH, Badal was so annoying. He sat right behind me and was forever running his hanky through his fingers. Apparently, he was the only one from the Very Cool and Hip People who was forced to sit in front because he made everyone LOL otherwise. Like now.

Everyone burst out laughing, while someone hooted from the back of the class. It had to be the Very Cool and Hip People. I bit back a retort and felt heat rise on my face. Seriously, what was everyone's problem? Fine. Ents it was.

The class broke up into different groups. I stood up and sat down again. Which group was mine? Raina stopped at Badal's table with the Very Cool and Hip People and said, "Savitri? What a fuddy-duddy name. We should call her Aunty." The flock obligingly sniggered. "Full aunty-type bag also."

What was that girl's problem? For the last few days, they seemed to be wherever I turned, ready with a sneer, a cutting remark, a grimace. I just couldn't figure what I had done to deserve this. Bullies. Mean, beautiful bullies.

I wanted to scream, but instead I turned and said, "Better than a Bollywood-type name any day."

Before Raina could respond, the same lanky boy

who had scooped up the fruit popped up in front of her.

"Hey! Remember me? We met on the grounds. I am Rushad. Come on—we meet outdoors." He jabbed a pale pink-painted thumb to make his point.

He began walking and I followed him, deliberately not looking at those Very Cool and Hip People. Morons. Meanies. "We don't have a room?" I finally asked as I realized Rushad really did mean outside. *Of course* we didn't have a room. Just my luck.

"The world's our oyster," he grinned. "Come on."

I scowled seeing Zainab, Trisha, and Amit head to the library for their book club meeting, and sighed loudly.

"You could have joined the chess club," Rushad said.

"I don't know anything about chess, except Knight to H3."

"Wow, you know your *Potter*, Savitri."

"I also know my *LOTR*, my precious," I said. "And it's Savi."

As we reached the grounds, I saw a pitifully small bunch of students gathered by my Tree. Yes, *my* Tree. Every lunch break I sat by Tree and felt like I had a friend. Suddenly, I didn't feel like a loser for being part of an eco club. Maybe I'd even learn some tips and tricks on keeping Dad's plants alive.

It was boiling hot already, a sharp contrast from the

morning. I pulled off my sweater and tied it around my waist. But it was too hot to keep it even around my waist, so I removed it and stuffed it into my bag, which was better especially as we had moved into Tree's shade.

"So, introductions?" said the boy. "I am Rushad, and I am president of the Eco Ents."

"Gia."

"Sana."

That's it? Three members? No wonder they had co-opted me. Gia looked a little scary, all confident with a voice that made me think of pebbles under a stream for some reason.

"Hi, I am Savi," I mumbled. I shifted from one foot to another.

"Samar! Uff! Hi, sorry, late!" Samar had come running to join us and was huffing and puffing a bit.

"So you finally decided to show up," Sana said.

Interesting, no one here seemed to like him.

"Sana," Rushad cleared his throat. "Drop it."

"I'm here, right? Now what did I miss?"

"Introductions." Sana clapped her hands. "Everyone, welcome aboard, and the last but most important introduction, meet *Ficus mysorensis*." She pointed at Tree and winked at it.

Weirdo.

"What's a ficus?" I asked.

Samar and Gia looked at each other and burst out laughing. "It's a fig tree," Samar said, turning away, shaking his head.

Why were they laughing? It's not like everyone knows the names of all the trees in the world.

"So, some housekeeping rules," Sana said, ignoring the two of them. "We meet here twice a week, Wednesday and Friday afternoons. The first rule—you do not talk about the Eco Ents Club. The second rule of Eco Ents Club is you do not talk about Eco Ents Club. The third rule of Eco Ents Club: We are trees, and the trees are us."

Quick, someone give me a cookie for not rolling my eyes. First, an introduction to a tree. Then rules. That, too, some mumbo-jumbo about trees and us. Next, they would ask us to hug Tree—which I totally was not doing.

"Come on, repeat after me," Sana said.

I waited for someone to go boo and point out it was all a prank. Nothing. I looked at their admirably serious faces. Even Cucumber Tendril Boy. Okay, and they repeated Sana's rules. I mumbled along, thinking that chess seemed way more appealing now.

I started as something banged against the trunk, barely missing my head. It was a volleyball.

I picked up the volleyball and watched Raina walk up to me. Instead of apologizing, she smirked. "You were in the ball's way."

"Were you trying to send it away from the nets? If so, definitely. Well played."

The Eco Ents laughed as Raina sneered some more and stalked off to join her set of fawning friends. I tossed the ball after her. There they were—the Cool and Hip Volleyball Club with their fancy sneakers and amazing sweatpants that never got sweaty.

Sana shook her head and opened a *dabba* full of cookies. Heyy, I do get cookies for not rolling my eyes. I took one and she beamed. "They're triple-stuffed chocolate chip cookies with palm oil–free chocolate, hazelnut spread, and a smack of sea salt."

Mmmm. It tasted as good as it sounded. As the cookies were passed around, Sana and Rushad droned on about meetings and seeds and plans.

Samar was kneeling, staring at a leaf on which a golden green beetle was perched. He held out his hand, and the beetle crawled on to it. I held my breath, even though I was not close by. A beat later, the beetle opened its wings and flew away into the canopy. I looked up again at the branches that seemed to reach out like an umbrella. Somehow, under Tree, the weather was just right, not too hot, not too cold. I looked away to find my clubmates staring at me.

"Uff, were you not listening?" Rushad asked. "We need your help. It's urgent." He looked disappointed, like I had grabbed the last cookie from the *dabba*. I had not.

"Oh." I suddenly felt cornered. I definitely could not look after plants if that's what the club did. And I couldn't manage any money matters; I was terrible at math. I definitely didn't want to recruit more members; I wasn't exactly a people's person. "I can . . . umm . . . what are my options?" I vaguely remembered Maharukh Sir saying they did gardening and more green bean stuff like beach and forest clean-ups and all.

"Well, we know . . . "

"You know what?" Shoot, did they know about Dad? How?

"That you can . . . you know . . . you can communicate—" one of the girls said. What was her name? Right, Gia. "There's a reason you were placed in this club. You know what we are talking about, right? We know."

No! There was no way they could know. *No one* could know. I suddenly felt breathless, was I getting a panic attack? I recited the names of Dad's plants in my head—aloe vera, jasmine, rosemary, black-eyed Susan, basil, papyrus, *kadi patta*, and I slowly felt my breath returning. Deflection. Best bet. "You mean, you want me to do communication stuff? Like posters, slogans?" I raised my hand. "That I can easily do."

They looked at each other. Rushad shook his head and started to say something but just then, a buzzing surrounded us. As we all turned to look up, a swarm of insects rose from the canopy.

"At last," Samar said.

"I can't believe it," Gia whispered. "They're . . . they're finally he . . . "

Fear coursed through my veins as one of them came closer. It was a wasp! I jumped up and waved my arms frantically. "WASPS! WASPS! EEEEEK! Shoo . . . we need to get away! I don't want to get bitten!"

Everyone roared with laughter.

"Wasps don't bite," Gia said in between giggles, waving her hands carefully, and the wasp followed her gesture and flew back into the canopy of Tree. "They sting. Don't you know that?"

I flushed. I *did* know that. But it felt like that wasp had been making for me. And why was everyone staring at me again?

The group burst into laughter again. Gia was snorting and Sana was holding her sides. Even Samar and Rushad were chuckling.

"Your face when that wasp came—"

"Oh, that dance you did! We should tell Dance Sir; he will be thrilled to have such a talented dancer."

"Bite! Wasps! Ha!"

I turned on my heel and stalked off, feeling like a complete idiot, but their hoots followed me out of the grounds. From the corner of my eye, I saw Raina and gang whispering furiously in a huddle.

"Savi, Savi, stop!" It was Sana, running up behind me. "Look, we're just having fun. You know sting-bite and all that. Come on, it *was* funny." She gave me a tentative smile and a pleading look. "Come back—really, no one means any harm. We really need you to come back—let us explain."

The purple frog pressed down on my heart and I clenched my fists. Either I was going to slap someone or burst out crying. But I wasn't giving these people the satisfaction of seeing me cry, so I lashed out instead. "You're just a bunch of tree huggers. The only thing less funny than you all are knock-knock jokes."

Sana's face crumpled and I felt a slight twinge. But before I could say anything, an arm slipped into mine. It was Raina. Not only that, she was talking to me. To *me*! "Oh, ignore these Chipko Movement people," she chirped as Badal appeared at my other side. "Come with us. Wasps are nasty. Everyone knows that."

Before I could say anything, I found myself being ushered into the canteen along with the Very Cool and Hip People. I didn't dare turn back and look at Sana. Otherwise I'd burst into tears.

Chapter 10

The Invisibility Cloak Is Shed

Quick poll: What's the worst?

    A) Being ignored

    B) Being sneered at

    C) Being very, very visible

For most of my life, I had been a regular kid—nothing special, unless you counted my ability to annoy Mom, but nor was I truly cringeworthy. But after Dad's death, I had aced the invisibility game. It was simpler than opening my mouth and putting my big fat foot in it, and revealing the many shades of my mean streak. "Better to be neither seen nor heard" became my motto.

I had assumed that after the episode of wafting me away in a perfumed breeze from the grounds, I'd be once again persona non grata with the Very Cool and Hip

People. But the next day, as I grabbed my *dabba* and headed to the tree, Raina hijacked me.

"Lunch time!" she smiled. From the corner of my eyes, I saw Gia, Rushad, and Sana. Rushad half waved a gloved hand at me but put it down when Sana glared at him. The three of them turned and walked off into the city forest, trash bags in hand. Clearly, they were going on a clean-up lunch walk, which was definitely not the most appealing plan. So instead, flanked by the Very Cool and Hip People, I headed to the canteen. I felt like I was part of a royal procession and almost expected one of them to wave as the path in front of them magically cleared.

There was of course Gorgeous Raina and Annoying Badal. Then there was Toffee (yes, that was his real name—I'd sneaked a peek at the class register to check), the one with all those stories peppered with the word "like" and an accent from his summer visits to the US of A and Lake Como, perhaps making him the only Shajarpurian who liked to travel. And lastly, but not least-ly, Mausam with her gorgeous hair, who could name all the cheeses available in a fancy gourmet store while describing their taste, smell, and aging process, and even the food pairings, with astonishing accuracy—all of which made me age a few years and kept me off cheese for a whole day.

And then there was Samar—at the edge of each table, the fringes. There but not quite there. I couldn't figure him out.

Oh great, we were stopping for an "ussie." Pouts, hair flicks, et al. I didn't know how to pout, or rather didn't want to, so I just stared wide-eyed.

"Give me your number," said Toffee. "I'm adding you to our messaging group." Phones were not allowed during school hours, but they were everywhere if you looked closely. I rattled off my number and felt a buzz in my pocket.

This was just bizarre. I genuinely did not know what to make of it and wondered what Chetna and Firoze would think. I had been taken under the Very Cool and Hip People's extensively perfumed wing. Which made me very, very visible. As we went down the staircases and up the corridors, heads turned, people made way for us. I immediately felt like I was in one of those mean, cool girl-type Hollywood high school films. Only we didn't have those cool lockers. Or cheerleaders. Or a tough-looking football team. All we had were the stares.

At the canteen, they sat at the best triangular table— right by the window—so the smell of vada pao and sambar wouldn't smother them. The canteen uncle nodded and removed the reserved sign from the table. I slid into a corner, awkwardly hunched around my *dabba*. Raina took prime spot, and Badal was right next to her, mopping up sweat with his handkerchief. Toffee was unwrapping a ham and cheese sandwich, while Mausam complained about the food in the canteen and the weather.

"The sambar's so sweet, and the coconut chutney so watery," she moaned. "I don't know how you can bear to eat it. Mumma always insists I pack food from home. And now it's raining. I hate the rain, it's so wet."

"It's really not so bad," Samar said, plonking his tiffin on the table and prodding her to move over and make room for him.

"Better than cold Maggi," I said.

There was a silence as everyone stared at Samar and me. I closed my eyes. Why did I say that out loud? I felt like Dad's cactus—all prickly and thorny, quick to hurt. The thing about meanness is that it has this eerie way of making one feel as small as an atom. My meanness made me feel even smaller, so small that I would have to crane my head to look up at an atom. But I still couldn't help it.

"Ouch!" Raina said.

"I happen to like cold Maggi," Samar said, opening

his tiffin box to reveal sandwiches. "But not peanut butter sandwiches. What am I, five?" He looked at my lunch box, which had masala rice, and said, "Swap?" Before I could reply, he had switched boxes and was digging into the rice.

I stared at him, but my lunch was rapidly vanishing. I reached for a sandwich with a sigh. At least I liked sandwiches. Also, it was either that or starve.

"So," Raina bent her head closer to me, "tell us about you, Savitri. Oops, I mean Savi."

My heart started galloping. I hated talking about myself because once you start, then people ask questions—questions that lead to answers about your father. I didn't want to tell anyone—even saying it out loud made it all too real all over again.

"There's nothing much to say," I mumbled.

"Oh, come on," Badal said. "Enlighten us. Where are you from?"

"Delhi," I said shortly, pushing away Samar's *dabba*. I was no longer hungry.

"Ah, the city of masks," Badal snorted elegantly. "Come here to get some fresh air, *haan*?"

"What fresh air?" I tried to change the subject. "The air's turning quite foul, just like Delhi."

"Ooh, maybe the smog followed you, Savi," Toffee

said silkily. "Maybe it's all your fault. Just kidding, chill! So tell us more, what does your family . . ."

I began ripping a tissue paper into tiny pieces. My heart was beating loudly in my ears, and I wondered if they could hear it. Why did they keep asking questions?

"I just remembered," Samar said. "We have an Eco Ents meeting now." Everyone groaned.

"They are the worst," Badal moaned. "They're always telling people to stop using plastic. Remember last year when I had got that keto diet delivery? They complained *so much* about all the plastic waste. Who cares?"

"Such dorks," Raina smirked. "You really need to transfer to another club—I can't believe you all waste your time with *phool-patti.*"

"I know, I know, what to do?" Samar said, pulling a face. "Come on, Savi. Let's go."

I gratefully packed my *dabba* and followed him out. But then he turned towards the computer room. "You're welcome," he said and stalked off.

Conclusion: C. Being very, very visible is definitely the worst.

Chapter 11

Keeping Up with the Very Cool and Hip People

After that day, wherever I turned in school, one of the People was next to me. Literally in my face. At home, my phone was flooded with some of the most inane conversations about food and memes and trending trends.

I was also grateful for it. The choice was between eating desolate, lonely meals in a scrubbed house, mucking around in the school garden with the weird Ents, or hanging out with my new, cool friends. It wasn't a difficult one. Also, it seemed to annoy the Ents, and that was a complete bonus.

But every time I came back home, I was exhausted and curiously deflated. The purple frog on my heart felt heavier and clammier, and no matter how much I laughed, how much I talked, it wouldn't move. Worse, I found I just couldn't say no to them. Every time they asked me to hang out, I'd end up saying yes, even though the last thing I wanted to do was go out. But it was better than the ghastly silence at home.

The People were constantly going to their favorite cafe at the beach—Past Food Nation—or having a jamming session or gaming evenings at one of their houses or going for long drives in town in their swanky chauffeur-driven cars. They even dragged me to karaoke once, and I *hate* karaoke.

At least I got to see a lot more of Shajarpur, the city my father grew up in. It was his home, the plants constantly reminded me. The more I saw of it, the more I felt connected to him—and to Tree, who was sharing so many of their stories. Theirs and Dad's. It wasn't like I missed him any less, but it was like finding the prequel of a favorite book and stumbling into the many stories that told me so much more about him. Things I never got to ask him.

A banyan tree showed me a young Abhay clutching his Baba's (my grandfather) finger as they tried to cross the road.

Baba was so good-looking—with his dashing beard and mustache and a fitted shirt and bell bottoms.

Eating golgappa with two boys and a girl under an Ashoka tree. Was that Aamir Chacha? It was!

Playing cricket on the school grounds, running furiously to catch a ball.

Fighting with Aamir Chacha under a baobab tree. Ouch, did he just swing a fist at him? Oh, he got one smack right back. Now they were laughing!

It was like being in limbo, a word that suddenly made sense to me. Neither awake, nor asleep, but I was much more present in another world. A world that made more sense than the real one. Sometimes I just stood there and smiled or bit back my tears. At other times, it was like a double take, as if I had seen someone I knew. Which I did. Or I would feel my world spin even if I was standing rooted to the same spot. I am pretty sure the Very Cool and Hip People thought I was some wool-gatherer, which was fine by me. I still felt so out of place in this city and with my new friends—like I was laughing too hard, talking too much, and being just a bit . . . extra.

Maybe it was because they constantly treated me as a school improvement project.

Raina once picked up a clump of my hair and said, "How about we go on a haircut date? My treat! Come on. We will get Sebbie to sleek up your hair. It's just so . . ." She had beamed at me, while spraying sanitizer on her hand, and I had no choice but to smile back weakly. Badal just sneered and then looked into his phone to see if his hair was still standing up. It was.

Toffee and Mausam would scan me from head to toe every now and then and say, "Are you sure you want to wear *that* to *this* place?" Immediately, I'd feel like this glob of amoeba, shapeless and insignificant. Why did they keep asking me to hang out with them if I was so obviously not one of them?

Also, it didn't help that they were all rich and hung out at cafes where the bill always ended up being staggering. None of them even blinked at the tab. And I was fast running out of pocket money.

Being around the People also meant that I was constantly surrounded by a cloud of chatter, which after the deathly stillness of home was taking a bit of getting used to.

Like today at Past Food Nation, I ordered the cheapest thing on the menu, which was an espresso. Not even a double espresso like the uncle who owned the place suggested I order instead. "Sure, not a double?" he asked, while swapping jokes with the People, whom he seemed to know very well. In fact, come to think of it, everywhere we went, they seemed to know the uncle who owned the place.

Luckily, the espresso came with a button of a biscuit which melted like a cloud on my tongue. I kept taking tiny sips to make the bitter coffee last for as long as possible, while they talked non-stop.

"Did you see the latest Autumn collection?"

"Yaar, that fuchsia top. Must. Have. Now."

"That bias cut just doesn't work on her—it makes her look like a building."

"I need another custard cruffin. Anyone else?"

Somewhere, a phone buzzed. Toffee looked at his phone and then at Raina and sniggered. This was another constant—messaging each other while they were right next to each other. The conversation continued, of course.

"I wish I was back in the Maldives. At least I could just dive into the waters any time I wanted. My uncle has an amazing seven-star resort there. We go there every winter."

"Did you try the new organic, grass-fed chicken kale quinoa salad at Chinchi? That mushroom aioli dressing is to die for. My aunt's the one who started the restaurant, you know?"

To die for—how easily people used these words.

"I felt like I was having a heart attack when Maharukh asked me that ridiculous question today. I mean, what was I supposed to say? As if I was even listening to his drone-drone voice."

"I know, right? I was listening and thinking I'd literally die if he called on me."

"You didn't, right? So shut up."

Okay, that I said out loud. Again. Worse, I'd said it to Raina. No one, ever, interrupted Raina. And they definitely did not tell her to shut up. The Very Cool and Hip People turned and stared at me. Samar looked like he wanted to say something, but instead he pulled out his phone and started typing.

I gritted my teeth and pushed my tongue against the back of my teeth so that I couldn't let another word through. I didn't want to apologize. People took heart attacks and death too lightly. There was a reason that the saying was "as serious as a heart attack."

"You are weird," Toffee said, raising an eyebrow. Everyone laughed and I felt the knot of worry dissolve inside me as I exhaled.

But my relief was short-lived. The bill arrived along with homemade chocolate fudge! Most restaurants give you *saunf*. And if they are feeling a bit generous, then it's saunf mixed with sugar crystals. But here it was cubes of shiny chocolate fudge.

"So we'll just split the bill six ways?" said Mausam.

But it was a rhetorical question. With a sinking heart, I saw her do the calculation on her phone. "Rupees 670 per person. Oh wait, with a tip, that's 700."

PAH! There went my plan to buy the new Green Humor book.

Chapter 12

Need a Hug

If things were strange at school, then in my plant life at home, they were just topping the horrendous-o-meter.

I returned home from Past Food Nation feeling all droopy and floppy. I dumped the key into my bag, took off my shoes and stuffed my socks inside them, all in one brown bundle. Meher loped in right then and I could see her judgy face. I grimaced and picked up the grimy socks.

"Don't you remember?" Meher said. "It was one big reason Mom and Dad would fight—Dad's sloppiness, and, well, socks. Like, Mom would come back from work and find that Dad had just dumped his socks inside his shoes."

I stared at my sister, my hands full of smelly socks. "Umm . . . no. Mom and Dad never fought."

My sister's face told a different story. "Duh! Of course they did. Over *so* many things."

"Maybe I wasn't there?"

But she was already opening the lids of the casseroles on the table to see what there was to eat. "You were," she said, breaking a piece of *kothimbir wadi* and biting into it. "Yelling 'Ewww, gross!' with me." She held up the piece of *wadi* and took another picture. "Home food's the best—especially when you didn't make it," she posted.

"They never fought," I insisted. They were the perfect couple, every one of their friends always said that. I tried hard to remember this, but I was pretty sure that Meher was making things up. I closed my eyes. I couldn't even remember Dad properly on most days without the help of his plants. In my head, he was just this towering presence, but I couldn't see his smile or hear his voice anymore.

I rushed into my room, shutting the door quickly behind me. My bag fell to the floor with a loud thump, the sound echoing my heartbeat, which sounded to me like ten bags falling to the floor every second (clearly Meher's dramatic reels were getting to me).

I ran to my desk, holding back my sobs, to that photo frozen in a white frame. Dad was not looking at the camera, he was staring lovingly at his jasmine plant. A giggle escaped me—of course he was. Mom was listening to a podcast as he gardened. I was only a toddler, wearing a hideous, frilly frock and clutching a toy pail and a shovel. Meher had taken the photo, and it was slightly out of focus. Like the photo, my memory was also out of focus. And in some ways, the photo didn't help—it just fixed his image in my mind but didn't bring back memories of him. How could I have forgotten what he sounded like? My mind raced and yet, it stayed obstinately blank. Like the time my computer had crashed, and I kept trying to switch it on. My mind was that black screen with a green line flashing on it.

I clutched the sides of my desk as the smell of jasmine wafted over. I stumbled to the plant, to where it sat by the window. It shuddered, even though there was no wind. The window was shut, and the fan wasn't switched on. The smell lingered, even though it was just a brown stub now.

I reached out and touched the plant with trembling fingers. "Please, please," I whispered. "Please let me not forget what he looked like." I felt the familiar pull into moss and luminosity, but this time I could also smell socks, the really foul socks that my father was holding. They were pink with gray elephants on them. Mom was backing away as he offered her the socks to smell. I was there with Meher.

"Arre! Abhay," Mom yelled. *"Put those socks in the machine."*

"You know, sometimes I wonder if you're talking to me or the kids!" He looked a bit angry.

A glare from Mom and he pointed at the brown shoes standing neatly on the shoe stand. "They're clean."

"No, they are not."

"See!" He sniffed a sock. "My feet don't stink."

"EWWWW!" Meher yelled. "That's yucky, Dad—stop it!"

"See!" Mom crossed her hands and stood there.

"Come on, I can wear them for two more days—why waste water by washing them?"

"That's disgusting, Abhay!"

I was too young to remember it properly, but as I found myself back in my room, I could still hear the angry voices fading. How could they fight in front of us? I needed a hug. Especially Dad's. He gave the best hugs—comforting, as if he was taking all the stress from your brain to his heart in that one hug. He smelled of comfort, a mix of fresh soil, leaves, and smoke.

Mom was exactly the opposite. Apparently, Nana-Nani, Masa-Masi, and the rest of her family were never very demonstrative. Mom's hugs = awkward. They were one-side arm squeezes, as if you were sitting in a bus next to each other and she was putting her arm around you so you wouldn't fall off the seat. Dad would demand a family huddle and she'd just scrunch up her shoulders and wait for it to be over.

Meher was kind of okay when it came to hugs, but her hugs were bony, and it felt like someone had put clothes (but really cool ones) on a skeleton in the biology lab and said, "Now go forth and offer comfort!" A quest at which, alas, she failed. But bony hugs were better than awkward side hugs. Though, it would be strange to dash outside and demand a bony hug—and there was a good chance she'd just ignore me like always.

I looked around for Bekku—she was always by the jasmine plant. But the one time I needed her, she was off chasing pigeons or doing whatever she did when we weren't around.

I left the house, grabbing an umbrella. It was raining again. I could feel Kulkarni Uncle's eyes on me from the vantage point of his ground-floor house. I mumbled, "Good evening, Uncle." Immediately, he looked pleased, shouting a cheerful greeting back.

Before he could ask me any questions, I kept walking. When it rained in Shajarpur now, the winds howled like sadness, and the rain was a torrent. Umbrellas were useless. A city that had never needed them was suddenly pockmarked with them. But they were no match for the storm rain. UGH, my umbrella turned inside out, the spokes sticking out like ruffled feathers. *Kaagdo*, Mom used to say, like a crow. I felt like that, bedraggled.

Finally, I was back at school, standing at its imposing, triangular brown gates. The school was silent because it was way after hours. Suddenly, I knew why I was here. I needed to see Tree. But how was I to get in?

A figure stirred from the shadows. I jumped. It was the security guard. She smiled and beckoned. I saw her every day, and she seemed to be loved by the Ents, but "Stranger Danger" flashed through my mind, and I hesitated.

"You want to meet Tree?" she said.

How did she know?

"Come," she beckoned again, unlocking the gates. I slipped in and watched as she locked it again. Was I going to be trapped? Would this woman kidnap or hurt me? I looked at her badge, which said her name was Pushpa.

"Go on, I am here," she nodded encouragingly, her

hand gesturing towards the back of the school. "They will like it."

Who were *they* now? Was there a gang waiting for me? Were they waiting to make money by kidnapping me just because I went to a posh school? Well, they'd totally be disappointed. But there was also something reassuring about Pushpaji's face, and I found myself nodding. I stood my mostly useless umbrella against the gate. It had stopped raining and was sickly warm now, my clothes stuck uncomfortably to me. I silently sidled off to the back of the school. I kept my hand curled up around my phone in my pocket as I turned the corner, ready to run back. But nobody was there. Except Tree.

As always, the familiar feeling of unwinding raced through me. The purple frog lessened its grip on my heart.

"Hi," I said. Great, here I was going in for a hug. But before I could roll my eyes at myself and change my mind, I stepped under Tree's canopy and put my arms around their trunk. Pushpaji was right. They, Tree, did like it.

Chapter 13

Fun Time with Fungi

If anyone knows how to give a hug, its a tree. We're solid and always ready to be held. Hence, the term tree hugger.

Its really like spring has come early.

There you are, visiting my world.

I hold the three worlds together—the air, the earth, and the understory.

There you are, stepping straight into my sturdy heartwood. Each ring is the keeper of the stories I have witnessed and recorded on them. Can you see them, hear them, smell them? Stories of heat and rain, droughts and forest fire, of death and life.

The underland of the soil is a kingdom of its own, an intricate tapestry of living networks. Complex and infinite, stretching for miles, reaching everywhere, holding everything together with its roots, like the many hands that came together to form a human chain after the last riots.

Step in, leave your fears behind. Let the lights guide you.

The rootlets, too numerous to even comprehend, each stretched out like fingers, covered by the luminosity that had taken over my imagination for so many weeks now. It was like a garden full of the tiniest fairy lights, moonlit pinpricks woven into nets. I almost expected an elf to pop out. But as I looked closer, I realized it was fungi, rows and rows of them, little light bulbs on top of the rootlets.

Tree was at the heart of a forest, where they were the most ancient, the wisest, the one that bound all the other trees together. The neem, the *pongam*, amaltas, *doodhi*, *tendhu*, silk cotton, jackfruit, jamun, mango, and even the newcomers—the gulmohar, the rain tree, jacaranda—they were all a family.

I listened deeply as the mycorrhizal fungal network was communicating, transporting nutrients and chemical compounds among the forests. I heard whispers.

Quit hogging my sunshine.

Ever heard of canopy shyness? You should try it some time.

The banyan on MG Road is gone. Made way for a metro. They passed on her nutrients to everyone on SV Road.

Let's have a moment of branch waving for them.

Got extra nutrients today? I am running short.

Here you go, take some from me. I have plenty.

Oye, that kiddo needs some air and sunshine. Kindly adjust that canopy—let them grow.

After a moment I realized what I was hearing. It was trees fighting, negotiating, sharing, responding—just like any other family. Just like our family. Just like how Mom, Dad, Meher, and I fought. It wasn't a din like in the canteen at school—it was a comforting whisper, like standing under a bamboo grove and listening to its many songs. But with its own grammar.

The ever-shifting soil is where our dead come to rest in earth and stardust. My earthworms, they extend their elastic bodies, making rubber band loops, burrowing deeper and deeper into the soil, raking memories that are buried and preserved by my underland.

Memories of Shajarpur. Its once-upon-a-time love for trees. Its bitter amnesia.

Its people. Its animals. Leaves, flowers, and insects. The living and the dead.
And your father.

Dad, who visited Tree when he was my age. Dad, who shared his world with Tree. And now Tree was sharing it with me.

I don't know how long I stood holding Tree. I felt like I had traveled across multiple universes. I should have been terrified, but strangely for the first time in a long, long while, I wasn't.

Chapter 14

A Deal Is Struck

I didn't know how to go back to Shakespeare when my whole life had turned upside-down once again. I hugged the magic close to myself. Wild magic! It was as if Dad had left me a story and now I had finally opened the book. All I wanted to do was sit with Tree and listen forever.

But next morning, there I was, listening to Amba Ma'am reading from *The Tempest*. She was floating around the room in her wheelchair, her blue dupatta wafting behind her like a cape. Did I imagine her shooting me a death glare? No, it couldn't be.

Our English teacher was usually quiet and contained, but open a Shakespeare play and, before you knew it, all the world was her stage. She flung about her arms, her voice echoed across the room, and she wheeled herself around the classroom, as if lost in a totally different world.

"GONZALO: The king and prince at prayers! Let's assist them, for our case is as theirs.

SEBASTIAN: I'm out of patience."

"Tch."

I jumped. That was the very annoying Badal again, who kept going "Tch" every few minutes, followed by a heavy sigh. And because I sat right in front of him, it was like this loud sound right in my ear.

"Tch."

I turned and glared at him.

"What?" he asked.

"Are you calling a dog? A cat? A goat? A pigeon? Tch, tch, tch? Because it's not working. None of them have turned up. So, really, quit it."

I turned back only to see Sana scowl, and Samar snort and stifle a laugh as Badal jabbed him in the ribs. Sana barely spoke to me now. She even pretended to not hear if I asked her something about class. But I had bigger problems to worry about. Like another death glare from Amba Ma'am. I hurriedly began mouthing the words along with her.

After class was over, Amba Ma'am asked me to stay

back. "So Savi, I believe you have been missing Eco Ents Club sessions?"

Oh no! Had Rushad or Sana complained? The *sneaks*. No, this had to be Gia's doing. I assured Amba Ma'am, keeping my fingers crossed behind my back, that I'd attend the meetings. Why were these weird tree-hugging club people telling everyone about my skipping? So uncool. I had already ignored Rushad when he had announced, "Club meeting in five, yo," at the end of class.

At the gate, even Pushpaji stopped me to ask why I wasn't attending the meetings. "They need you," she said.

I bit my lip as the rest of the students streamed out of school. "Look," I said. "It's really none of your business." I immediately felt terrible. She'd been so kind to me yesterday.

She smiled sadly. "You know, I had a daughter your age. She was just like you—willful. Never listened to anybody. I understand, though. Why would you listen to me? But all I can say is think about it. The club really needs you."

I wanted to apologize, but Pushpaji had already turned around and was ushering the younger students to the school bus. Each one was holding the other's shirt and had their fingers on their lips. It made me think of Dad picking us up from school. (Mom used to be on school drop-off duty.) But it had stopped when Meher insisted we were old enough to take the bus.

Speaking of the devil, there was Meher with her friends. It was astonishing how they were all clones of each other—perfect hair, skin, enunciating each word. I opened my mouth to ask if we should go home together but, just then, one of them broke away from the group and raised her phone. The others put their left hands up, began wiggling, and broke into a dance as "Single Ladies" boomed from another phone.

I watched open-mouthed as they danced in sync. Nobody else seemed to be bothered, except for Pushpaji, who had her hand in front of her mouth, clearly trying to suppress a giggle. It was all over in thirty seconds; everyone high-fived each other and began to troop out. "We are going to my uncle's this weekend," one of the clones was saying. "It's going to be awesome. He has this huge home theater system. Meher, you *have* to come."

Sighing, I turned to the parking lot where the Very Cool and Hip People waved me over to their fleet of swanky, shiny cars. I felt so relieved just to have someone to wave back at. Just as I joined them, Sana marched towards me. Uh-oh.

"Come on," she said. "Eco Ents meeting." She crossed her arms and stood there, glaring at me.

"You don't have to go," Toffee said, turning to Sana. "You can't order her around." Raina nodded and held my hand. Mausam and Badal huddled closer towards me. Somehow, that did not make me feel better.

Sana was not done though. "I can complain to Maharukh Sir that Madam here has been skipping club meetings. Let's see what that does to your assessment. Even Samar's attendance is better than yours."

"Sneak," Raina said. "Savi, we don't listen to sneaks. And that, too, freak sneaks."

Sana looked at me, then turned and walked away.

I suddenly felt guilty. Okay, the club had been mean, but they had apologized, and the attendance did count towards my final assessment.

"*Yaar*, I better go before she complains. But I'm going to ask Sir if he can shift me to the Crossover Sports Club." I squeezed Raina's hand back and let it go. Then I winked at the others, "Chill, I'll go show my face. No biggie. Anyway, it's time to head home, so you guys leave. I'll talk to you later."

As I left, I wondered who I had transformed into, this person who winked at people and tossed around phrases like "no biggie." By now, most of the other students had gone home, and it was only club members on the grounds. The purple frog on my heart always felt slightly lighter when I saw Tree. They were just the most magnificent being in my world. But today, Tree looked tired, a little droopy—just like I felt.

A whole battalion of people surrounded them, including Pushpaji, Amba Ma'am, and Maharukh Sir. Even Samar was there, looking deeply uncomfortable. I wanted to turn and run away but Amba Ma'am saw me. She smiled. "Look who made it."

I was greeted by the sullen, scowling faces of the Ents. Maharukh Sir cleared his throat.

"Look," Rushad said with a sigh. "We're sorry. We didn't mean to laugh at you."

"Or scare you," Sana quickly added.

Oh, they seemed sincere. Before I could say anything—

"It was just . . . you said the wasp would bite you." Gia looked like she was going to laugh again, but Pushpaji frowned at her. "I'm sorry, really," she added, waving a peace sign with her fingers. "Look, we need you at the Eco Ents Club. Please come back."

"You need me? Really?" I wished I was one of those people who could raise an eyebrow ironically. Like Dad. But in spite of having spent countless hours in front of the mirror, it was not a trait I had mastered. Though I *had* inherited his caterpillar eyebrows.

"What for? So you can make more fun of me? Or because you want to tease me about the fact that I have a thumb that's browner than Delhi's smog? I can't keep any of our plants alive at home, they are all dy . . ."

Rushad was clearly trying hard to not grit his teeth when he zeroed in on what I'd said. "You have a brown thumb?" He waggled his blue glitter-painted thumb.

I shrugged. Samar, meanwhile, was whistling to a red-vented bulbul who was trilling merrily back, oblivious to everyone else.

"We can help you," Sana said carefully. "We're all excellent gardeners. In fact, we all learned here, at the club."

"Yeah, we can help you take care of your house plants. Just tell us which plants you have and send us pictures, and we will tell you how to take care of them," Rushad offered, graciously. Everyone nodded.

I suddenly felt a surge of hope.

"In return, you have to attend club meetings," Amba Ma'am said. At least this time she didn't shoot me a death glare. "Deal?"

Sana held out her fist.

They seemed sincere enough, but could I really believe them? They'd *really* help me save the plants? Plus two teachers were here and even the school's security head. Either way, I didn't have much of a choice. I fist-bumped Sana, and then everyone joined in.

"Deal."

A wasp buzzed from the tree, and I almost jumped. To their credit, none of them laughed. At least not out loud.

Chapter 15

Don't Give a Fig

Fact: Never had I ever climbed a tree.

No thank you. Not interested. It's fully unnecessary.

But here I was, standing under Tree. My Tree. All right, Tree was special to the Ents, but I needed them more today. Anyway, Tree spoke to me, not them.

I sat back down on the root and immediately, I stepped into that loamy, luminous world. I heard a whisper.

Ever seen—
  a smiling tree?
  a laughing tree?
  a tree that's so delighted
  that their heartwood sings?

Fine, stop tossing poetry at me, I will climb up. Bekku can climb trees, so can I. I could totally do this. But why, I cursed, had my parents not taken us tree climbing? After ages, it was a gorgeous Shajarpur day— crisp, like a perfectly salted potato chip. I surveyed Tree—the left branch seemed low enough. I grabbed it and stepped onto a root jutting out of the ground.

Okay, so now I was stretched across the tree trunk like a bark gecko. Only I was very, very visible. Why could I not have camouflage superpowers?

Tree, help?

Silence.

Lovely.

I put my foot a little bit higher, hauling myself up to the next branch. The branch held. I pushed myself up, but my foot slipped, and I scrambled for a nub or branch to rest on. Nothing. There was nothing but air! I felt like a cartoon character as I slid my foot up and down the bark, trying to find something. No, no, nooooo!

Just then a hand steadied my foot, and I was hoisted on to the branch. I scrambled and gripped it like my life depended on it. Given I was three feet above terra firma, I knew it was a slight exaggeration, but still.

I looked down—Samar was standing there and grinning. "You're welcome," he said, putting his arms on the neighboring branch and swinging up just like the monkey he was. Effortlessly—it didn't even muss up his hair!

"I was doing fine," I said, gingerly putting my back to the trunk and settling in a bit more comfortably.

"Yes, I could see. You were just fine—like a proper cartoon. Only thing missing was the soundtrack of *tada tara tadaaaadeee tadeee.*"

I scowled at him, watching as he climbed higher and higher. Finally, he sat on a branch diagonally opposite me, legs dangling in the air and, to my utter surprise, took out his phone, put on his headphones, and started listening to music.

"Excuse me," I said. But Samar was bobbing his head. A black and red butterfly was jauntily perched on the side of his head, opening and closing its wings. It looked like he was wearing a butterfly clip. I waved my hand but neither Samar nor the butterfly paid any attention.

Fine, I didn't need the company, I had come to talk to Tree. I touched Tree, but the traitor sat stubbornly silent. Hello, I wanted some Dad memories, but clearly Samar sitting here meant I couldn't tune into Tree Channel.

Sighing, I looked up. It felt a little like being in a storybook world where anything was possible. I reached for my backpack, but I had left it on the ground, along with my book, snack, and water.

Oh well. I looked around me. An army of ants was marching up and down the bark. I put a finger in their path and smiled as they marched around it. Sitting there felt like a hug, as if I was safe from everything and everyone—and from that frog on my heart.

It had been a few weeks since the Ents and the teachers had made me resume club meetings. Meher was often out late with her friends and she disappeared on the weekends, while Mom refused to come out of the room when she was not cleaning. Saying there was too much paperwork, she even ate her meals inside, which meant that if I didn't go out with the Very Cool and Hip People, I was left to eat all my meals alone in front of the TV.

Once again, I found myself gnashing my teeth, and I slowly unclenched them. My jaws had begun to hurt from all that gritting. Don't know why Mom didn't realize we missed her, and she was still there, with us. Shouldn't she be like a parent, fuss around us, look after us? But no, she was always BUSY. Work, paperwork, depression. Something was always more important than us.

"It's finally fruiting, you know," Samar said. I looked at him from the corner of my eyes—his headphones were around his neck. *Now* he wanted to talk to me. "It had stopped, but the wasps are back, pollinating the fruit, dying inside it, and . . ."

"DYING?" I almost fell off the branch. "They die? *What*?"

Samar was trying hard not to laugh. "You don't know?"

"Clearly!" I would have crossed my arms indignantly, but I needed to hold the trunk tight.

"So," Samar said, touching a bulb right next to him, "there's something unique about these ficus trees. They don't pollinate the usual way of seedpods and all. No sirji, not good enough for us. Instead, each tree species has a wasp unique to it." He smiled slightly as one came buzzing by, as if she knew she was the subject of our conversation.

Samar held out his hand, palm facing the canopy, and the wasp settled on it lightly. I was pretty sure he called it "Tina" softly.

I think my eyes were as round as a wasp's nest. He was very weird.

"Ever wondered why you never see fig flowers?"

Before I could shake my head, Samar continued, "It's because what you're seeing is not exactly the fruit. Think of them like inside-out flowers, and a whole bunch of them together. That inflorescence smell attracts female wasps. So in goes the wasp, into the fruit, to the tree that's just hers. They leave their eggs inside all the flowers."

"How do they get in?" I asked, in spite of myself. I couldn't help staring at a fruit-which-was-also-a-flower bunch.

"Look at this one closely?" As if listening to him, the wasp flew over to me. If I had even the faintest clue how to climb down, I would have gone right away. But instead, I took a deep breath as the wasp settled on my arm. I got goosebumps.

"See the inverted teeth and special hooks on her legs? Isn't she beautiful?"

I totally disagreed but decided it would be impolite to voice that to a member of said flying, stinging, easily-dying species perched on my arm. I nodded instead.

"She loses her wings and her antennae to get in, her first sacrifice for her young ones. Then the second sacrifice, for the tree. After that, of course, she cannot leave."

"You mean these fruits are full of dead wasps?" I spoke a little too loudly. The wasp buzzed off, and I couldn't help but think she sounded indignant.

"Well, not exactly, the fig fruit contains an enzyme to digest them." He stopped to look at me. I was completely grossed out.

"Hey," he said softly. "It's nature. Let me finish. Then,

well, the eggs hatch, and there're larvae which feed on the fig and well . . . okay, it gets worse before it gets better."

I shook my head but didn't say anything, and Samar took it as a cue to continue. "The males, you know, fertilize the females, bore tiny exit tunnels, and die. And then the females leave the figs, carrying pollen. They travel—and how—and then they go on to the next fig fruit. All of this in just a matter of days!"

"This is the worst story I've ever heard."

"Depends on how you see it," Samar said. "It's a mutually beneficial system. The females have a safe space to lay their eggs. The tree gets to travel without going anywhere and, at the same time, they become more trees. And because it's not bound by other pollination rules, it fruits almost through the year. Chow time for us and lots of birds, animals, et cetera."

"UGH! I don't think I'm ever eating figs again."

Samar shook his head. "Without all this happening, the world would actually have a lot less biodiversity. Because the fig trees kind of are like the big sisters of this world, they ensure that the plants and animals thrive."

"But they DIE!"

"The wasp doesn't know if its life is for two days or 100 days or 100 years," Samar said. "They live those two glorious days without thinking of it as short or long.

It's life as they know it. A complete life." He sighed and touched the bark. "Tree? Tree is the holder of death and life all together."

Before I could respond, the branches above us shook and I stared open-mouthed as a big gray bird settled there. I winced. Big bird = big poop. But since I was stuck there, I hastily shut my mouth. After all, why offer a soft target? It was a strange bird, S-shaped with a curved beak that looked too big for its body.

"She comes here almost every day," Samar said. He was looking at the bird with a sad smile on his face. "One of the many birds who depend on this tree. Her mate died—I don't know what happened. But they would come here together and sit together every day. And then one day, he wasn't there."

"Maybe he found someone else?"

"Hornbills mate for life, Savi," Samar said.

The bird opened her beak and let out a loud wail. It was such a sad sound that my eyes welled up. I wanted to wail with the bird. But there was not a chance of that happening in front of Cucumber Tendril Boy.

The three of us sat companionably on the tree until the bell rang. Samar scaled down quickly and looked up at me. The grin was back on his face.

"Need help?"

I shook my head even though I couldn't begin to figure where to put my leg to come down.

"It's all right to get help sometimes, you know," Samar said. He pointed to a small protrusion in Tree. "There, just put your left leg here and then jump down."

Heart hammering, I did as told. I landed with an inelegant thump. But instead of laughing, Samar held out his hand and hoisted me up.

The hornbill shook her feathers and took to the air.

"Shall we?" Samar jogged off without waiting for an answer. The butterfly followed him. He stopped, turned back, and scowled. "Also, it's all right to help someone if they ask you for help, Savitri."

Chapter 16

I Swear . . .

If you were to put me under oath, I might have to confess that I was beginning to enjoy gardening and being part of the gardening club. Not that I'd admit this to the Very Cool and Hip People. Or even the Ents.

After the attend-club-meetings-or-else episode, I had gone home and sent photos of my plants to the Ents messaging group.

Rushad: That's aloe, just leave it be—it will be fine.
Gia: How much water have you been giving the succulents?
Me: Umm, twice daily?
Gia: NOOO! STOP! NOW. 2/3 times a week should be enough.
Me: Two or three?

Gia: *eyeroll emoji* Do two right now because it's cold. Three times a week for the curry leaf plant.

Sana: Your jasmine plant seems like a write-off.

Me: No.

Sana: Fine, fine. You need to keep pruning the roses. Also, that black-eyed Susan. Water it only when the soil feels dry.

Me: Umm?

Rushad: Touch the soil.

Me: Oh. I did. Now?

Rushad: Savi!

Cucumber Tendril Boy: Wash your hands.

Rushad: Samar!

Gia: Oi, move it into the sun. Why is the black-eyed Susan in the shade? *shrieking GIF*

Rushad: Pushpaji gave you that magnesium packet—did you use it?

Me: What to do with it?

Gia: Really, you need to take notes. Forget it. We will make you a plan.

Sana: You mean I will, and you will all take credit.

This meant that the Ents and I had arrived at an uneasy truce after the last meeting. I started ignoring their eye rolling and weird jokes. The detailed plant schedule they had drawn up for me—which ones to keep in the sun, when to water each plant—it had all worked miracles, and if I could break into dance like my sister, I would have.

Meanwhile the Ents meetings were all work and no talk in a way that Tom Sawyer would totally not have approved of. We met twice a week after school at the forest by Tree. Maharukh Sir, Amba Ma'am, and Push-paji dropped by occasionally, offering advice or a packet of seeds or a story.

I was working on the school vegetable bed, spray-ing neem oil on the leaves. It was one of those now rare Shajarpur days, where the weather was just right again. I was enjoying the sun on the back of my neck, and some-thing loosened within me as I inhaled the many smells around me. I braced myself as visions of people protest-ing by a construction site swam in front of me, followed by another vision of a shadowy group of men sitting in a boardroom. UGH, why was I seeing all this? I only wanted to see Dad stuff. Plants were supposed to be com-forting and all. It was getting so hard to do anything—to eat a salad without seeing where the rocket leaves came from, to walk on a leafy floor without it giving me vi-sions of things that had happened in the neighborhood, or to take care of the plants without them flooding me with memories of our family when it had been whole.

The last one I didn't mind. The others, their intensity was increasing. It had gotten worse since I had hugged Tree. Serves me right for wanting hugs.

Still, visions aside, I was really enjoying spending time with the school plants and Dad's green babies (huh, that made them my siblings). Just loosening the soil, watching the chili plant flower, seeing a new leaf unfurl on the fern, it all made me feel more real, like I was doing something tangible. I could see why Dad had been obsessed with gardening.

Rushad began singing softly, and I turned to look at them all.

He was seriously like a plant charmer—any plant bed he worked on seemed to thrive, turning into a riot of bright colors. He was patient and worked so quietly that he was like a chameleon camouflaged in his beloved plants.

This was unlike Gia, who was constantly jabbering until she gave us all a headache. She had a special affinity for wasps and bees—good for her! I always maintained a three-foot distance from her. Social distancing FTW.

Sana was just so solid. It felt like this motley crew would fall apart without her. She mapped out schedules, knew just when saplings had to be transferred to bigger pots, and brought goodies for everyone.

Samar promptly ate all of these, stealing mine if I wasn't looking. He seemed to love the earthworms and the beetles and would spend hours staring at a spider or a bark gecko, and they seemed to love him back. The Pied Piper of Bugs and Birds and Bats. I mean, there was a fly chilling on his finger right now. A fly, yuck! He made a soft sound and smiled. But I did notice that he was very different when he hung out with the People. It was like Samar's alter ego attended these club sessions.

Seeing that I had paused, Rushad stopped singing. He turned beetroot red and said, "Savi, got a minute?"

Sana, Gia, and Samar stopped their work and turned to us. I felt like I couldn't breathe. Why were they looking at me?

"We wanted to tell you something," Rushad continued.

"Look, Raina," Samar said.

Rushad turned to him and scowled, "You are hanging out with them too much, really. Calling me Raina of all people!"

"No," Samar's lips were a straight line. "Raina . . . there."

Raina, Badal, Toffee, and Mausam were sauntering over to us.

"Samar, Savi, my uncle's scored us tickets to

Razzle D's show tonight—come on. We have just about enough time to go home and change," Raina said, coming up behind me. She wrinkled her nose at the smell of the neem oil and added, "And shower." Mausam took out a bottle of perfume and sprayed it all over her, while Toffee removed the bug spray from his pocket and held it in front of him like a talisman.

I wanted to say that I had to finish the work I had been assigned, that I didn't like live concerts, that ever since Dad had died, even walking into a crowded space scared me. But I could not. No one said no to Raina. I got up and wiped my hands on a piece of cloth. Even Samar got up and joined them.

"Oi, that's my scarf," Gia yelled. She snatched it back and glared at me.

"Shoot! I didn't know, I . . . I . . . didn't mean to . . . I was just . . ." I stammered.

"Oh, just go," Gia said. But then she handed me a bottle of neem oil and said, "For your plants."

I stood there, torn between wanting to apologize to Gia and joining the Very Cool and Hip People who had started walking away. But Gia had already gone up to Sana and was whispering something fervently.

"Coming?" Badal stopped and asked.

I had already ruined it here. No sense ruining it with the only friends I had. Razzle D it was.

***

A week after the scarf-wiping episode and several days of ominous silence on the Ents' messaging group, I geared up for the next meeting. I was late because Bhansali Ma'am had asked me to switch off the lights and fans on the entire floor. I ran down the staircases and to the grounds where there was a full-fledged club meeting going on.

I slowed down. None of them were looking at me. They were all peering into Tree's canopy, as a swarm of wasps danced above them. I quickly moved back to a safe distance and then dove behind the big hibiscus bushes near Tree. Thankfully, the wasps hadn't seen me—or at least I hoped they hadn't. I peered out from my safe place.

The Ents had been the ones in one of the raked-up visions, to whom the wasps had spoken! I should have realized this sooner. What in the world was happening? And how had I landed splat in the middle of this grove of teenagers? And what, Tree was dying? I struggled to remember clearly. No no, Tree could not be dying.

"The wasps are very clear," Amba Ma'am was saying. "You've got to talk to Savi. For the last two years, Tree has not been communicating with you all."

"Yeah," Gia said. "It was a silence that was scary—even more than the tons of Hindi homework Bhansali Ma'am set us today."

Everyone laughed, but Pushpaji spoke up. "Just as Savi joined school, the wasps appeared again. It's not a coincidence—we knew Tree was waiting for someone for a reason. Gia, we need to tell her and explain why it is urgent."

"Pushpaji, I keep trying to," Sana said. "But I don't know how to talk to her." She pulled out a box of food from her bag, and my mouth watered as I saw that she had brought cheese-chutney sandwiches for everyone.

Samar stopped staring at the insects to add with a sigh, "People, we have to be a little careful. Look, we have had Tree in our lives forever. Since nursery. We've kind of always accepted the talking-buzzing Tinas—it was just, you know, as normal as the watery sambar in the canteen. We're so used to this. But for Savi, this is all new."

"Thanks, Smarty Pants," Rushad said with a scowl. "If you know her so well, then you talk to her, no? You both hang out with your Raina and Badal and all."

Samar held up his hand. "Hey, that's not fair."

"Stop it, both of you," Sir stepped in. "All we know is that she's apparently a very important person."

"You mean a very impudent person," Gia said.

"BUT WHY!" Rushad said. "She barely talks to us, she walked off from the last session without even an apology, and she's friends with the people who hate us. And this after all that we did for her plants! I vote we chuck her out and apologize to Tree." He shrugged and tossed a cricket ball in the air, catching it neatly. "Enough ya, let's just say tata bye-bye." Rushad was red with anger, as rare a sight as a flock of great Indian bustards.

"We can't," yelled Gia. "The wasps are very clear. Tree's also very clear. Don't you get it? Tree's weakening. The weather is turning here, the climate is changing, people are forgetting as Tree weakens. We need to stop it before it's too late. We need her. Enough."

"We don't know how exactly we need her. Tree's not telling us anything," Sana said.

They all glared at Tree.

"Well, I don't know, but Tree says that only she can help. Thanks, Tree."

A lone wasp buzzed out of the swarm.

"Tree just said 'You're welcome,'" Gia explained. Everyone started laughing. Tree's branches quivered, the leaves shaking, and the wasps rose up in the air to dance a merry dance.

I realized I was trembling. The purple frog was pressing down on my heart as if it could still the frantic beating. I stayed behind the bush until the Ents went home, my mind jumping from one conclusion to another. What did they want to talk to me about? Why was I an important person? Even thinking that sounded ridiculous. The only good thing was that my tree-talking skills were clearly matched by Gia's wasp-chatting talent. It suddenly made me feel less alone. But also, there was something else. I just wasn't sure what.

Chapter 17

Which One's Lavender?

"Whoa!"

"Don't you ever knock?" I scowled at Meher as she barged into my room, Bekku in her arms. She looked shocked, like the plants were suddenly talking to her as well. But it was really because Dad's plants were thriving. My room looked like a little rainforest. Every corner was bursting with flowers—red, yellow, pink, and violet. The windowsill was lined with pots from which spilled shiny, glossy leaves—dazzling greens, purples, mauve. The aloe vera had grown so much it looked like a monstrous zombie trailing along the floor. I watered the black-eyed Susan, and immediately—

A whirring seedpod
*   Its fate cemented*

I sighed and looked at my sister instead.

"It must be this weather," Meher said, taking a deep breath. The sweet smell of basil lingered in the air alongside mint and lavender. It was a little overwhelming, just how much was happening in my tiny room.

Bekku jumped out and headed straight to the jasmine plant. As usual. It was really a wonder that she didn't break its brittle brown branches. But she was always careful to curl around the plant without hurting it.

I glared at her, pulling off my headphones. "Yes, because clearly I haven't done a thing. There's magic, na, in this air. Magical Shajarpur, where the air is clear as crystal, the water purer than the purest of glaciers, where plants miraculously heal." I waved my hands as if casting a spell on the plants. "What spell must it be? 'Mumbaca Dabra'? Or maybe 'Fee-fi-fo-flump, help this plant be tall and plump'? If you haven't noticed, the weather here is starting to suck as well. But yes, let's thank the climate."

Meher put her hands up. "Sorry, baba, sorry. I didn't mean it like that. I think they look wonderful. Peace?" She walked up to a caladium and touched its pink and green leaves. "How gorgeous these colors are! Look! The pink matches my lip gloss!" She picked up her phone, and I immediately protested, "Don't you dare dance!"

She laughed and took a pouting photo with the plant

and shared it on her social media feed. (Proud of my #GreenthumbedSister!)

I ignored her, concentrating on removing the weeds from the jasmine plant. The still-brown jasmine plant. Some leafy plant with tiny yellow flowers had decided to grow itself in each pot and now needed to be bid farewell to before it throttled all the other roots. Or so the Ents had told me.

I tried shooing Bekku away, who predictably did not move. So I picked her up and plonked her on the bed. "She's always eating up the plants, chewing up the grass, and whatnot! I'm pretty sure she killed my lemongrass," I told Meher.

I glared at Bekku and then felt terrible as the cat walked up to me and rubbed her head against my knees, purring loudly. I sighed and patted her before turning back to my plants. It hadn't been the poor cat's fault.

"Can I help?" Meher said softly, twirling her finger around a leaf. She sounded nervous, which was very unlike her.

"So now you want to help? Now that they're thriving?" I growled, tugging at a weed viciously, but I stopped when I saw Meher's face. I remembered Samar's parting words. Damn, Samar.

I fingered a brown leaf and an image of a family picnic

at Lodhi Garden swam in front of my eyes. *Dad, Mom, Meher, and I were playing a game of cards. Of course, Mom was cheating as usual.* It struck me that Meher looked sad and pinched as well. I immediately hated myself.

"Hey." Meher came and stood next to me. "It's not been easy on me either, you know. These plants make me think too much of Dad. I couldn't bear to see them without him. But now I feel guilty. Ever since we moved, you've spent most of your time taking care of these plants. And none of us have helped you."

I bit my lip. "You can loosen the soil in the lavender." Meher waved her hands in front of my face and wailed, "Nooooo, my nails!"

Exasperated, I handed my sister a small spade. Meher took the spade and stared at the plants.

"Uff!" I was trying hard not to laugh. "That plant, there. The one that looks like grass. No, not that, that's a money plant. How can you not tell the difference? Oho, Meher, that one!"

"Careful!" I warned my sister as she began attacking the soil with as much gusto as she approached a bottle of nail paint.

For a while, we worked side by side silently, as I added compost to each pot. I wondered if her reels had almost been an escape for her for the last few months—like the plants had been for me. The jasmine plant shuddered, and a sweet, sad smell filled the room. "Emotional black-mailer," I muttered to it.

"How did you learn all this? Dad would be so proud," Meher said, now poking at the soil tentatively and wrinkling her nose at a spider web on the neighboring plant. She hastily moved to the other side of the pot. "I mean, you had a brown thumb too. Like Mom and me. Remember how Dad always kept trying to get us interested in gardening?" She sighed and then said, "Let's face it, if there was an earthquake and Dad had to choose between saving us and his plants, I often wondered who'd win. I can just imagine him saying, 'But they don't have legs to run like you lot.'"

I smiled. That totally sounded like something he would have said. "They've forced me into this stupid club at school," I said. "It's called the Eco Ents Club. They're a bit mean—and they talk about me behind my back. But they do know their gardening." Even as I talked, I felt my face tug into a smile, when I really should have been rolling my eyes.

"I'm confused—they're mean, yet they help you?" asked Meher. "They're the ones you meet over the weekend?"

I paused. Meher meant the Very Cool and Hip

People. "No, they're different," I said. Very different.

She finally looked up from the plant and said, "Hey, what would you call a lavender plant if it shriveled up?"

I shrugged my shoulders.

"Lavender Brown!"

Chapter 18

P Is for Progress

The next day, as the students of Vriksh Samosa School settled into their seats, the intercom crackled, and the principal's tinny voice wafted into our triangular rooms.

"Good morning, Vriksh School! Welcome to yet another day of learning and wisdom."

Samar shook his head. He opened his notebook and began to doodle a brain sprouting like a fountain. I smirked and opened my geography textbook for a last-minute revision before the test.

"We're delighted to say that this Diwali and Eid vacation, students will get five more days off."

The class broke into cheers and began thumping their desks. Amba Ma'am tried to shush everyone.

"A Very Big Company will be cutting down the tree at the back of the school, and the noise may disrupt classes. So the Parent-Teacher Association agreed that it would be best to extend the holidays and . . ."

Did I hear that correctly? I looked at Sana and saw her face fall. I turned to see Rushad look even more disappointed than usual. He began chipping at the green nail paint on his thumb. Samar had stopped doodling—his hands were clutching the pencil hard.

"Did she just . . . ?" Sana whispered.

"Sshhh . . ." Amba Ma'am flapped her hands. "Listen."

"The tree cutting is important for progress. Economic development. Social development. Can't you all smell the sweet aroma of progress? Thank you and happy holidays."

With that, the intercom shut off. Amba Ma'am looked horrified and after throwing a nervous glance at us, she zoomed out of the classroom. The chatter went back to its usual decibel levels, but my ears were still echoing with the principal's announcement. I jumped as I heard a snap. Samar had broken his pencil in half. Sana leaned towards him, but he shook his head. "Later," he scribbled on his notebook.

Next was geography class. I was pretty sure I failed the test even though it had questions I actually knew the answers to—I just kept making silly mistakes.

The moment the last bell went, the Ents stood up as one and walked out of the classroom. I followed them quietly. The weather matched our mood perfectly. It was dull and gloomy, clouds rolling over our heads. At last, we reached Tree. I immediately went and touched their massive trunk. I felt the need to be close to them.

Immediately that same vision of a board meeting sprang up in my mind. There was a room full of shadowy men in suits, kurtas, dhotis, veshtis, and safari suits . . . and I could see two women as well. They all looked thrilled.

This again! I snatched my hand away. Why would this not stop? I only wanted Dad memories.

I could hear the Ents talking frantically behind me.

"Did you hear that?"

"Did she mean our Tree?"

"How dare they do that?"

"It must be illegal!"

"What's for lunch?"

Everyone turned to stare at Gia. "What? What happened? I'm hungry. I just came from a dentist's appointment," she said.

Rushad filled her in.

Like the others, Gia quickly lost her appetite. She

was glaring at all of us like we were a bottle of insecticide aimed at wasps. "Tree knew, that's why they were sending us all those messages. To act urgently. That's why they wanted us to talk to Savi . . . "

"To me?"

Suddenly, the Ents remembered that I was also there. Group death glare! Ouch.

"Why are you here now?" Sana asked hotly. "Go away. This is all your fault."

"Yes," Gia said, speaking so fast that it was hard to follow what she was saying. "You with your 'Oh, help me with my plants, but I am too cool for you' attitude. It's fine when *you* want help, but if we even try to talk to you, you have to go for a concert it seems. This is really on you."

I looked at them blankly. It was true, I was not the most disciplined of club members. I felt a twinge of guilt because for the last few meetings, I knew that the Ents wanted to talk to me, but each time I had made an excuse and left early. I was terrified that I would end up blurting out everything I was seeing on Tree Channel. "I don't understand. What did I do? I mean, I can go to talk to the principal, but I doubt she's going to listen to me."

"Or anyone, really," Rushad said. "But that doesn't

mean we shouldn't try." He coolly turned away from me, making me feel like I had been doused with insecticide. He nodded to the group. "Let's go?"

"Don't we need an appointment?" Sana asked.

"No, she has an open-door policy between 3:30 and 4 p.m.," Rushad said.

So, at 3:25 p.m., the Eco Ents, Amba Ma'am, and Maharukh Sir stood outside the principal's office. I hovered at the edge, while the tired assistant kept telling everyone to sit down or wait outside because there weren't enough chairs. "*Kay re*, end of the day *itna magaj maari*. Don't take so much *traas*." The phone rang and she waved us in. We backed up against the wall as a group of uncles walked out, patting each other's backs.

The Ents stepped into the cool, woody confines of the principal's office. I slunk in behind them, feeling like a proper shady shadow.

"Yes?" Mrs. Pankhida asked, looking at us over her glasses. They were hooked to a shiny chain around her neck, which glinted in the brown, wooden room.

No one spoke. It was deathly quiet.

"Yes?" she asked again, now frowning at us. "What is it?"

Gia elbowed Sana, who jumped and said, "Ma'am . . . we . . ."

"Yes?" She steepled her fingers and looked at Sana intently. When Sana didn't answer, she looked at the two teachers.

Amba Ma'am cleared her throat and said, "Ma'am, about the tree . . ."

"Ah yes, wonderful, isn't it? Progress."

"Progress?"

"You heard me once. Please don't repeat what I'm saying. I do not like it when teachers and students don't pay attention. This is why you come to school. To pay attention to things. To learn. For wisdom."

Before she could launch into a speech about the school's motto, Maharukh Sir spoke up, "Ma'am, but what sort of progress?"

"The capital P kind," she beamed at everyone. "The only kind."

"But why do we have to cut Tree down? Can't we have Progress with them . . . I mean, the tree?" Sana spoke up finally.

The principal frowned. "I don't understand, what is the problem? The tree is dying anyway."

"Ma'am, we don't think the tree should be cut. It's a very old tree—do you know how many years it has lived?" Maharukh Sir plucked at his mustache anxiously.

"Oh, my teachers and my students! Don't teach me

history, I can tell you more history than you've lived in your scant lives. Out with the old and in with the new, I say. We must allow for Progress. Yes, see that's what the letter says—it's imperative for Progress for the tree to be cut down. Or else, we will be standing in the way of Progress and that wouldn't do, would it?"

With that, she dismissed us as a pair of parents raced in, swearing that their child had not done whatever it was that they had been told he had done.

"So that's that?" asked Gia, as we walked away.

"How can that be just that? We will protest. We will start a petition. They can't just cut a tree in the name of progress. Even if it's with a capital P," I said quickly. I couldn't let Tree . . . no. No *way*. The purple frog was pressing hard on my heart.

"Ahem, they've been doing just that in case you have failed to notice so far," Samar replied. "Not just here."

Seeing my expression, he said, "Will you listen to us now?"

I nodded slowly. Was this a terrible idea or was this a terrible idea?

The Ents stumbled back to the grounds as if magnetically drawn to Tree. The teachers clapped them on their shoulders and left.

I took a deep breath to say something, anything, but

the club members had turned away from me. They were staring at Tree again. As one, they gathered and formed a triangle around Tree. Rushad pointed at an empty space, I assumed he was beckoning to me to step into it.

I felt like a member of some cult. I had heard about such groups—they lured you in and then practiced strange rituals and all kinds of things. I was suddenly petrified, and I wondered if I could leave somehow. Would they notice? All right, if they started chanting, I was out of there. Tree's fate be damned. Sorry, Tree!

I looked around me. The last bell had gone ages ago. The grounds were completely empty. I suddenly remembered that I had told Raina I'd go to her place. Oh well.

"Savi, it's high time we tell you something," Rushad said.

"Wasn't our decision," Gia said. "It was the wasps who insisted we do."

"Shush," Sana hissed.

"We know," Rushad said, frowning at everyone else. He turned to look at me. "We know about your grief, your loss."

I stared back at them, my heart suddenly very still, as if the purple frog had swallowed it whole. "What . . . how? Have you been spying on me?" Rage ballooned inside me. *How dare they?* All thoughts of Tree being chopped down were pushed away at once.

"We don't know who it is," Samar said quickly. "We know you also have lost someone. Like all of us." He gestured towards all the club members. "A loss—it leaves a mark."

I touched my face. Was there some sort of a mark there, visible for everyone to see? An ugly gaping scar, like the slash of a claw? I stared fixedly at Tree. I couldn't bear to look at the others. I couldn't bear to see their faces filled with pity, telling me to be strong and resilient or some such gibberish. That would change everything, just like it had in my previous school. Chetna, Firoze, all of my friends had started looking at me differently once Dad had died. Like they were very sorry for me.

I dreaded that look. And those words, the hollow words that everyone—my teachers, the parents of my friends, and all those busybody uncles and aunts who had come for the cremation—said: "Time is a great healer," "Death touches everyone," "You are young, someday it will feel less sad," "Stay strong for your Mummy." None of them got it. None of them. I could not bear it. Every time that hollow pity came my way, I slashed at it with words. Made it shrivel with a look. Until none of my friends knew what to talk to me about. Or even how to come up and say hello. Until my teachers just glossed past me in their classes. Until I finally left that school and city behind. Leaving my friends behind along with their pity and hollow, empty words.

And now the pity would raise its ugly head again. My knees buckled as I crumpled to the ground. I closed my eyes, reached into the mud, where Tree's roots lived. I felt the earth stir beneath me gently, and Tree's rootlets surrounding me, as if holding me tight. A light shower of leaves enveloped me. My fists slackened as a hand covered my left hand.

"Savi, we know what it feels like."

It was such a gentle, not-judgmental voice that I opened my eyes. There were no roots holding me tight, there were no leaves showering me, but I still felt comforted as if Tree had just hugged me. Of all the Ents, it was Gia who was holding my hand tight, like she would never let it go. "We know, not exactly, but we've all lost someone. Someone close to us. Someone who mattered."

There was not an ounce of pity in her eyes. I took a deep breath and looked up—my clubmates were looking at me with concern, but not pity.

A fruit fell from the tree and rolled towards me. "Go on," Gia said. "Keep it—it's for you from Tree." I reached out for it and clutched the fruit hard in my fist. It sat there, warm and very real. Immediately, I knew. *A small boy laughing as he played cricket with Samar; Gia and a kindly-looking old woman walking to the park; a young girl arguing on a bicycle with Pushpaji; a disease that gripped both Amba Ma'am and her sister.*

My breath caught. It was all too, too much.

The Eco Ents Club sat down, this time encircling me in the triangle formation.

"I lost my kid brother," Samar said, looking up into the tree's canopy. He could not bring himself to look at the others as well. "Cancer. It was so *quick*. One moment he was being my annoying younger brother, trailing my friends and me, wanting to bat with us, and the next moment, he was in the hospital, filled with tubes and all. He never came back home." He took a harsh breath. A butterfly fluttered on to his arm, but I don't think he even realized it.

"Ammi," Sana said softly, clutching her hands tightly together. "Accident on the highway."

"I don't remember my parents," Rushad said. "They were killed in a bomb blast on a train. I was just two years old." His hands were shaking as he spoke. "I live with my Nana and Nani, who are awesome by the way." He pronounced that last sentence fiercely.

"We know, we know," Samar said. "We adore them

too. Especially Nana's sweaters. You know he knitted a whole one for Tree as well?"

Sana sighed, "Samar . . ."

Gia said, "My nanny, she was amazing. She took care of me like no one else ever has." Her face was as white as bleached coral. "I miss her every day."

We had run through the Ents and there was a pause. It was not an awkward one. It was a pause. An exhalation. I noticed that Amba Ma'am, Maharukh Sir, and Pushpaji had returned.

Amba Ma'am said sadly, "An illness, it took my sister and left me alone. Maharukh lost his partner to COVID-19. He was something else, a force of nature."

Maharukh Sir didn't say anything, he just looked at Tree, but his Adam's apple was moving as if he was trying not to cry.

Pushpaji said softly, "I lost my daughter. She was born with a hole in her heart. My only son is in the village."

A silence followed all these revelations. I knew it was my turn, but how could I?

"You don't have to," Pushpaji whispered.

I finally forced the words out from under the frog's weight. "My dad . . . that's why we moved. Delhi had too many memories—or at least my mother thought." The purple frog shifted slightly.

"Are those his plants?" Samar asked.

I gave a slight nod. Gia gave my hand a squeeze and let it go to hand me a bottle of water. "Drink. You will feel better."

"Each and every one of us," Rushad said, "has been chosen by Tree. They speak to us through the fruits, through the wasps."

"Ahem, they actually speak to *me*," Gia pointed out, smugly. "I just translate for the plebs."

Maharukh Sir smiled slightly and shook his head. "Not now, Gia," he admonished gently. "Rushad here, he's got magic in his fingers—any plant grows under his care."

I had not imagined it then! But how was it real, how was this happening? There was magic in this air! Oh and Dad, he also had the same magic. I should have known.

"Sana, she just knows what each one of us needs and what each plant needs when. She is truly the glue that keeps the Ents together." I looked at Sana, but she was looking intently at Tree's roots. She was so not used to being the center of attention.

"Of course, you know Gia's talent," Sir said. "And Samar, all the other pollinators and the earthworms feel safe around him, which is why they are so comfortable around him and communicate with him. They have their own language."

That explained the mantis, the butterfly, all of them, being attracted like magnets to him! That was a talent I definitely was glad not to have. I wondered what the grown-ups' talents were, but I couldn't ask. Or maybe now that they had grown up, they had found other ways to deal with their losses?

"Nature is an old magic. One of the word's origins is," Amba Ma'am said, lost in her world of syntax and grammar, "from the late fourteenth century, an art that creates marvel with hidden natural forces. It's not a sleight of hand or trickery. It's nature. And trees! Why do you think trees exist in all myths and legends? Because they are the center of the magic. We don't know how it works, it just is." She paused and continued, "And Tree's been choosing us for generations. It's like a fierce kind of love. A love compounded by grief. It's that feeling that binds us together."

I found myself nodding. I understood that.

"There is something about loss, which makes you really see the changing world outside—the trees turning old and gnarly, the seasons changing steadily, the glorious short-lived flight of the butterfly, the whirring seedpod hitting concrete, a flower that blooms for one night, a steadying, dizzying reminder of the world that goes on, and our place in it," Amba Ma'am said.

"But you . . ." Sir stepped in, "seem to be import-ant. We don't quite know why. We don't get it. But Tree insisted."

I think I knew. I saw Gia looking hard at me—maybe she had an inkling as well because the wasps must have told her. But suddenly, a terrible thought came to me. "Are you saying Tree talks to ghosts?" Horror was totally not my scene.

"Bro, no, no ghosts, spirits, djinns, witches!" Gia said, shaking her head vehemently. "This isn't some fan-tasy series we're stuck in. If we were, I'd be the first one running out of here. Actually, no, Samar would be. He's the scaredy-cat among us." Samar stuck his tongue out at Gia as everyone laughed. I couldn't help but chuckle as well. "Nothing of that sort, okay. It's something else. Can't you feel it if you listen hard enough?"

I could. I didn't have to listen hard. I constantly sensed the power of Tree, a gentle, steady thrum, rever-berating across the school, under the highways, the steel flyovers across the sea, a coming together of all beings, not a noise but a feeling cutting through the concrete. It was like looking at a rock covered with velvety green moss. Only this time it was the whole city covered by the tree's roots, connecting it to another tree, and another, and another, until they were all holding hands under the earth, talking to each other, sharing losses and joys, propping each other up. Keeping the city alive.

It was such a relief to know that I wasn't the only one who felt this, who knew this. That there were others connected to this power, part of Tree's network, supporting all of us. That there were other teenagers who understood how sucky things were, and who didn't think I was weird for being able to listen to a bunch of trees and plants. Actually, I didn't think they knew the whole thing, so maybe I should just wait and see what they thought I knew.

I felt like I was going to burst with feeling so much. My expression must have given it away. "Yes, we know," Sana said, wistfully. "And they are not even at their most powerful."

"Tree is weakening," Rushad said with a frown. As he even spoke the words, a feeling of helplessness washed over us. It made me tremble.

"What do you mean?"

"The wasps have been dwindling. Their numbers are going down at an alarming rate. Trees are being cut down everywhere, that means our city's climate has taken a turn for the worse."

"I know—" I said. But everyone was too taken in by the enormity of what was happening to listen to me.

"And the most frustrating thing is we are still trying to piece it together. It's all down to four letters, really," Sana said. "TLEU."

Rushad cleared his throat.

But before Sana could continue, I spoke up, "Do you mean TLEU (ATA)?"

All pairs of eyes turned to me. It was their turn to look stunned.

"How . . . ?"

"You knew all along?"

"Dude, so not cool. You are back to being Savitri in my books."

"Who told you?"

I put up my hands, trying to calm the tirade down.

"Let her talk," Pushpaji admonished everyone. "Who told you, Savi?"

I looked up and pointed. "Tree did." I reached out and touched their trunk and . . .

Chapter 19
TLEU (ATA)

Uncle no. 54 coughed twice. All the other uncles (and two aunties) immediately quietened and sat slightly straighter on their plush, ergonomically designed chairs.

He surveyed the boardroom with beady, watery eyes. He folded his hands, "Welcome, welcome, my friends and family. Today is a special day. Today, we have finally moved one step closer to our dream." All the uncles (and two aunties) began drumming on the long wooden table on which a bonsai stood. Uncle no. 35 rang an ancient brass ghanti, Aunty no. 2 blew a conch, while Uncle no. 67 banged a spoon against his gold-rimmed chai cup. It was truly a landmark moment for The League of Extraordinary Uncles (And Two Aunties), also known as TLEU (ATA).

Set up in the early 1900s, The League of Extraordinary Uncles consisted of some of the most powerful uncles who made some of the biggest decisions about the country and the world. They were uncles who knew the right people behind banks, industries, real estate companies, film studios, governments, media houses. Not the actual CEOs, chairpersons, or trustees. They were the silent uncles, whose names never appeared in newspaper headlines or scandals. A whisper here, a nudge there, and entire forests were felled down to make way for mines and roads, banks decided which coal company to invest in, and malls came up where beaches stood. In the mid-2000s, they had admitted two aunties—Aunty no. 1 (no relation to Bollywood) and Aunty no. 2—to their India branch, in an attempt to be more diverse and inclusive.

Across the world, not a soul outside these elite groups knew about TLEU (ATA). When a certain Jan Havesomemore stumbled upon the League, he was dubbed a hipster by an Instagram influencer, and no one took him seriously again. When Ms. Doorander began asking nosy, inconvenient questions, her identity was deleted from the Internet, her social media accounts vanished, and she was reduced to a Nobody Knows Her—a fate worse than death in today's times.

Power oozed out of every crevice of the boardroom. It smelled of cold steel, new money, and iron left out in the rain for too long.

"At last, TLEU (ATA) has the upper hand in the Tree-son Project," Uncle no. 54 was saying. "The tree is wearing down, its hold is finally weakening. This city will soon be ours, and that tree will be felled at the altar of Progress."

It had taken decades. But it had been worth it.

At first, TLEU (ATA) had tried wreaking havoc on Tree by:

Poisoning its roots—the tree vomited it out.

Petitioning for it to be cut—denied, it was a heritage tree.

Trying to get someone to cut it down in the dead of the night—some hooligan wasps attacked the axe-wielder.

Trying to get someone to drill copper nails into its trunk—the same hooligan wasps attacked the nail-wielders.

No one and nothing could touch that &^*$%# tree!

But then, one uncle—Uncle no. 34—had seen a TED Talk about trees by some tree scientist and had said, "This tree cannot survive alone. It is connected to other trees, which makes it strong."

Uncle no. 34 had tried to explain the extensive root network that connected trees across Shajarpur, and that there were fungi that helped them communicate with each other, but all the uncles (and two aunties) had fallen asleep listening to him. When they had woken up and re-fueled themselves with adrak chai and filter kaapi, they unanimously agreed that the best way to launch the Tree-son Project would be to attack all the other trees in the city.

Slowly, over weeks and months and years, TLEU (ATA) got permission to cut down trees everywhere. East, west—it did not matter. Mangroves, rain trees, baobabs, laburnum, banyans, bael, breadfruit, tamarind, cassia, copper pod, peepal, flame of the forest, jamun, jackfruit, mango, margosa, and so many more. All gone.

Soon, the tree cover in the city diminished by 43.35 percent, making way for more roads, highways, train sheds, malls, flyovers. As it did so, the tree weakened. Its family was decimated, one by one, and TLEU (ATA)'s fat wallets grew fatter.

The tree was finally dying, which got them permission to cut it down. Of course, permission only came with the promise of building an Olympic-sized swimming pool at the very spot. A pool party, Uncle no. 78 had said with a snigger.

"I'm so glad I thought of it," Uncle no. 54 said, pressing the stray white hairs on his forehead down. "Such a good plan it was." Uncle no. 34 grimaced as Uncle no. 54 continued, "Soon the tree will be properly dead." His ample belly jiggled with laughter.

Chapter 20

Capisce?

My recounting what Tree had shown me about TLEU (ATA) was followed by an appropriately long silence from the Ents and the grown-up Ents. At least no one laughed at me or accused me of making it all up. I suddenly felt tired and light at the same time. It felt like I had been trekking with a rucksack that weighed a ton and had finally been able to put it down. It was a relief to tell everyone what I had been seeing, all those shady boardroom meetings, those conversations of people who thought they were entitled to destroy everything that came in their path, including Tree's memories. Well, almost everything. Some memories were too private. I hadn't realized that keeping this all to myself had taken a toll. This was, phew.

"I don't get it. How is this happening?" Rushad was

frantic. Samar got up and left but nobody noticed or cared.

"So you knew what TLEU (ATA) were hatching?" Gia asked. I did not appreciate her accusatory tone.

"Hey, hey, I thought I was imagining stuff, okay? How was I to know that all of this was real? Also, apart from the fact some of the uncles looked really familiar, everything was just a bit blurry, and I couldn't make it out completely."

"But . . . but . . . how can one group of uncles . . ." Rushad said, sounding confused and angry.

"And *two* aunties," Sana added.

Rushad continued, ". . . cause so much destruction?"

"*Arre, yaar,* we've known they've been chopping trees," Samar said. He was back with an armful of rolls and milkshakes. "Here, there's paneer and aloo."

"Ewww, I don't want paneer—all veggie food is always paneer!" Sana pulled a face and took an aloo roll. "So wrong. What happened to, umm, you know, the other veggies?"

Samar held one out to me as well. I was starving, so I took it and bit into it. With some food inside me, I could get to other pressing questions. "I don't understand either. How can this tree-chopping exercise make this much of a difference? Trees are cut down all the time."

Tree shook and a swarm of wasps came buzzing out, and I immediately blurted out an apology.

"Now you have ticked Tree off too—well done!" Gia said, who was clearly no longer in the let-me-hold-your-hand-and-comfort-you phase. Her moods were like climate change—unpredictable.

"Gia," Amba Ma'am said, shaking her head. "Who is going to explain? Sana?"

Sana sighed but before she could, Samar spoke up. "Let me," he said. "Savi, here's how it works. Trees are breathers of carbon, keepers of water, generators of food, givers of shade, homemakers to many beings, spinners of joy." He was speaking slowly as if he was talking to a child. I narrowed my eyes, but it had zero impact. "Too much carbon is baaaad for humans. And what happens when you cut trees? Poof! There's more carbon in the atmosphere. Less inhalation of carbon by trees, more carbon in atmosphere. That means that there is less water stored in the soil. Less food. Less places for birds and animals and insects to live in or chill in. Life is a *maha* bore—bad for the air, the water, the soil, the animals, and people."

Tree rustled. "Nerdsplainer," coughed Gia.

"Oh, and bad for trees," Samar hastily added. "Capisce?"

What did he think I was? A five-year-old? I wanted to pull a face at him, but that would perhaps reinforce that age impression. I settled for sarcasm. "Thanks for the EVS lesson, Samar. #TIL, #SMH. But how can this happen so fast?"

"There's this wise human," Rushad said.

"Yes, yes, you!" Sana agreed. Everyone laughed.

"No, really! I am talking about Suzanne Simard. She's a tree scientist! She's so cool, she studied this underground network of forests and discovered something amazing. See, there's the Internet, right? This worldwide web, the www, that connects everyone digitally. But the natural world already had that. It's called the Wood Wide Web now, but trees have always been connected to each other. It's kind of like holding hands. Don't eeewww me. Trees don't have sweaty, snot-filled fingers. What they have are roots—roots that connect to each other underground using fungi and bacteria. This means they talk to each other, share food, and even fight. Yes, they fight too. You should read Suzanne's research—she's the one who wrote about it and that's how we know about it. She's my hero."

"Tree-cough-fan-cough-boy," said Gia.

Rushad was in such a frenzy that he didn't even hear her. "Oh and our Tree, they are the Mother Tree of Shajarpur, kind of like the central hub. Apart from helping seedlings, sharing nutrients, all of the awesome things they do, Tree also harnesses their power to regulate our city's climate. Oh, close your jaw, Savi."

I couldn't believe what Rushad was saying. I had seen, heard, smelled, felt all that. Not just read it in a book or on the Internet or heard about it in some podcast or TED Talk.

"And the earthworms, they create wormholes in the soil, memory tunnels," I whispered. "Raking up memories from one tree to another, sharing, listening, forever."

"JUST LIKE THOSE SCI-FI MOVIES!" yelled Gia. "You know, you know, right! Those wormholes and time travel and all. It's so cool! I talk to wasps. You travel through memory. These people . . . umm . . . they cheer us on." She nodded at all of them and waved her hand regally. "Minions," she whispered.

Maharukh Sir sighed loudly.

Sana shook her head and said, "Savi, you see, the trees are all connected. The Wood Wide Web, it connects everything and everyone, which is why when one tree falls, it rips a little hole in the universe."

"Just like . . ." Rushad started to speak and stopped.

"Just like when someone dies, it rips a hole in our universe," I said. It finally all made sense now. Well, almost.

"But then why are all the people suddenly droopy? They like all this, na? Shiny, new buildings in place of trees, industries where forests stood, and dams stilling all rivers."

"Well, isn't it obvious?" Gia said. "As the connection weakened, the climate slowly began to change. We are only feeling the impact now. The only way that rip . . . that hole, starts, well, not to heal but to feel less jagged is through nature. It's all we have. And it's a lot!"

"What rubbish!" I couldn't help but say. "Is it really?"

As if on cue, it started raining and we all ran for shelter.

Chapter 21

Face-Palm Moment

As I reached home, my phone pinged. It was the Very Cool and Hip People group.

Raina: *Kids Kan Kook* marathon at my place?
Toffee: I am in. Shall we order in ramen?
Badal: Yes! Past Food's making a quinoa ramen now. Totes in.
Cucumber Tendril Boy: Bringing my appetite. But not for quinoa.
Mausam: *ramen bowl emoji* *chef emoji* *TV emoji* *running emoji*
Raina: Savi, you in?

I ignored the messages. I couldn't even begin to understand Samar—how could he be so chill when Tree was in danger? I opened the door and there was Mom, armed with a lint roller, following Bekku, who was walking from one sofa to another. Something had to be done. Yes, yes, about Tree. But also about Mom. Really, this was getting out of hand.

I pulled out my phone, played the *Pink Panther* title track, and stood back. Everywhere Bekku stepped, Mom was brandishing the lint roller on the surface to pick up the black hair she was shedding. Now it was the perfect Insta reel, and poor Meher was missing filming this for her 8,723 followers.

Mom turned to me. "What?"

"What . . ." I asked back. "Are you doing? Let it be, na? Our sofas are dark anyway—no one will notice."

"I will!" Mom said hotly. She suddenly noticed I was soaked through. "You are completely drenched—and dripping water everywhere. Now go take a hot shower, put your shoes to dry, and everything else in the machine. There's *dhokla* in the fridge."

She looked so irritated that I followed her instructions to the tee. Why was everything so UGH? The purple frog on my heart was having a field day, bloating and bloating. But it just wouldn't burst. But well, at least there was *dhokla* to look forward to.

I opened the fridge and saw that everything was

arranged in military fashion. The lady's fingers were sitting in one line in a box, individually cleaned and wiped down, the *methi* had been dried with a hair-dryer and put into *dabbas*; the eggs were all laid pointy tip down and the tofu packets smelled of handwash. It must have taken her hours! I looked at the *dhoklas*. Had she used a ruler to cut them? They were as sharp as diamonds.

Every time I turned, I saw something squeaky clean. And we had a *lot* of stuff, so it wasn't easy.

The bathroom towels were lined symmetrically, the plants were constantly being adjusted to stand in one line, and if I spilled water while watering them, I had to mop it up quickly, or Mom would dissolve into her own puddle of tears. Everything had to be in its place. Really, if Mom was given a whistle, she'd be a fabulous PT teacher, keeping everything and everyone in straight lines, and making every day Sports Day.

In fact, ours was the only house in Builders' Building that never got complaints about trash segregation. Kulkarni Uncle, Damodar Uncle, and Das Uncle were always being given lectures by the Green Committee on what was dry waste and wet waste.

I filled up a plate, ladled a copious amount of coriander-mint chutney and *lahsun* chutney, and sat

SAVI AND THE MEMORY KEEPER 163

down at the dining table. Bekku immediately jumped onto the chair next to me, eyeing my food. Mom had mopped up the floor, though I had told her I would do it. She was now scrubbing the window ledge where pigeons kept popping by to add poop art on the railings.

"Mom? Mom? MOM!"

She turned with a start; her glasses were way down her nose, her hair bundled up with a gray-white pigeon feather stuck in it like a little fountain.

"I had a question," I said.

Mom pushed back her glasses with her arm and went back to scrubbing. "Hmm?"

"Why did we move here?"

"What do you mean? I've got a great job here—you know that. Especially in this economy. And the climate and water, so good. I mean, it's still not as bad as everywhere else. And not to forget, no rent."

"It's got nothing to do with Dad?" I asked.

Mom froze and then began scrubbing vigorously again. "How do you mean?"

"Mom, Mom. MOM! Tell me, please?"

There must have finally been something in my voice that made her put down the rag and come inside. She washed her hands, dried them, and stood behind a chair.

"This city is where I met Abhay," she said, a ghost

of a smile flitting on her face. "I had come here for an inter-college competition."

"A *what*?"

Mom laughed and sat down on the chair. "You won't believe it, but in drawing. I used to draw cartoons, and I wasn't half bad. And your dad, he was in the JAM event."

"He *jammed*?" I couldn't believe it.

"*Arre*, no," Mom reached out for a *dhokla* and a bowl and started crumbling it into pieces. "I mean JAM, the Just a Minute extempore contest, where you fished a subject out of a bowl and had to talk about it for a minute."

Of course I knew what JAM was. But I didn't want to interrupt Mom—what if she clammed up again?

"He got economics," she giggled. "He changed it into this whole thing on the debate of environment versus economic growth, and governance and policy, and the idea of social justice and equality—before we knew it, we were hanging onto his every word.

"And in my competition, I ended up drawing a whole array of politicians and trees having a tug-o-war, with the trees losing the battle. We both won and when my entry went up on the board, we were both standing right there, and he turned to me and asked, 'What's your favorite tree?'"

"NOOO!"

"Yes, can you imagine? What a terrible pickup line! And I didn't really know any trees, so I blurted out gulmohar. And I got a whole lecture on how climate change is making gulmohars blossom early, and had I noticed it and so on."

"And you still married him!" Meher had just walked in and was drinking in every word, just like me. She picked up Bekku and settled down on the chair. Bekku looked super annoyed and jumped lightly onto the table next to Mom.

"Let's just say, he over-elmed me with his charm. And I 'fell' for it."

"Ewww, that was a terrible one, Mom," Meher said, stealing a *dhokla* from me. Why was no one getting their own food? There were heaps of dhoklas in the regimented refrigerator. "So acorny of you."

"Such a face-'palm' joke, Mom," I jumped in.

"Not you too! I am treemondously stumped!" Mom said.

All three of us were giggling helplessly, cleaning and trees-in-peril forgotten temporarily. Pun marathons were a family tradition, and we hadn't done one since Dad . . .

Mom's shoulders were shaking with laughter as she switched on her laptop and began showing us photos. There was Dad—yikes, he was such a geek! And Mom, she was so young and carefree. They were standing by . . . *wait*, WHAT. That was definitely Tree.

"Mom," I said as she was clicking away. "Mom, MOM!"

Both Mom and Meher turned to me.

"Go back, that tree . . ."

"Hey, that's our school tree," Meher said. "The one Savi's obsessed with. Or rather in lurrrrve with. She's always hanging around it, I think she even hugs it or something."

"Well done on recognizing it," I said. "Mom, when was this?"

"Really? It's still there? Wow, it must be a zillion years old by now. Oh girls, this was Abhay's favorite tree. He even insisted I meet it." Mom rolled her eyes and then suddenly looked all giggly. "He proposed to me right after, under this tree. Not down on his knees and all, he made a picnic and right there . . ."

Mom went on but I was no longer listening. I knew it—that boy with the cycle, on the tree. Tree had some answers to give. It was Tree-Time, folx!

Chapter 22

Distraction, Destruction

I left Mom and Meher to the remnants of the *dhokla* and chutney and went into my room. I needed to clear my head. As usual, Bekku slipped in and curled up on the brown jasmine plant. I tried to recapture the lightness I had just felt but a sense of dread had crept over me. Dad's plants were starting to droop again. They looked as miserable as the Ents. I couldn't understand it, they had seemed fine—glossy and green. Now it was as if they were wilting before my eyes. Damn it, my brown thumb was returning! I didn't like this. I had worked too hard on keeping them alive.

I walked up to the zombie aloe vera. Nothing de-feated that one. It grew and grew. I touched its scaly, smooth leaf, and sigh . . . lights and that loamy smell enveloped me. I was back in the boardroom. I detested it so much.

Uncle no. 54 was feeling quite pleased with himself. His bulbous nose was twitching with joy. He could smell victory—it smelled of fresh jalebis right out of the kadai. He looked sideways at Uncle no. 17, still so fit with just a small paunch. But he was fooling no one with that comb-over. Wisps of candy floss hair were stuck to his shiny bald pate. He smirked.

Their plan was working. At a nod from him, Uncle no. 34 stood up and pressed a button on the remote control in front of him. The sleek TV sprung to life and words filled the screen—"the Age of Distraction."

He pressed the button again and the screen filled with chocolate bars, toffees, hard-boiled sweets, jelly beans, lollipops—it was like the outlet store at Charlie's Chocolate Factory. He beamed and said, "Children. They're so easily distracted. Hence, the phrase 'taking candies from babies.'"

He clicked the button, and a gurgling baby showed up on the screen. "Anyway," he continued, "they suffer from environmental generational amnesia. Every generation's children see the environment they are born into as normal. So the faster we clear trees and mangroves, reclaim coasts, the easier it is for them to think this is nature. You cannot miss what you don't know, can you?" He laughed. "And to help that forgetfulness, from last month, we've been steadily releasing a stream of entertainment across the country." The fine print on the slide credited a Peter Kahn and a Thea Weiss.

A schedule pulled up, fully packed like a student's day is packed with school, tuition, and hobbies.

"The video game, Metropolis Boom or Bust, *has been a runaway success. Children can't get enough of it. And it's not only children, but also adults. Needless to say, it has not been a bust." He smiled, but no one smiled back. Harrumphing, he continued, "The release of the super-duper hit film* Achchha Bachcha Log *is smashing all box-office records. Critics are calling it the 'ultimate family film,' and everyone and their uncle (ha!) is going to see it. Well done, uncles." Everyone patted each other on the back. One of the aunties cleared her throat. "Yes, yes, the aunties also," Uncle no. 34 quickly added.*

"This week will see the launch of the next season of the much-publicized web series, Yeh Lo G, *a first of its kind high-school drama. It's already notched the highest number of social media followers and it's only increasing."*

"Next," Uncle no. 34 paused dramatically, but he heard no audible gasps. Everyone seemed to be sending forwards to each other or shoving fistfuls of chivda in their mouths.

He knew this because none of them had put their phones on silent mode, and their phones kept pinging and the uncles (and two aunties) kept nudging each other, all to the tune of the crunch-crunch of moving mouths. "And let's not forget that we will drop Razzle D's newest album."

"Drop?" Uncle no. 2 looked up from his phone, as did Aunty no. 2. "Why would you drop it?"

"That's what the kids call it."

"Call what?"

"The release of a new song or a trailer," Uncle no. 34 said, who had done copious research on not only teen lingo but also social media trends, hashtags, and celebrity gossip.

"Why would they call it a drop?" Uncle no. 2 looked completely baffled.

"Moving on," Uncle no. 34 continued hastily. He didn't know why it was called that. He only knew what the social media captions said. "The Kids Kan Kook *road show will be flagged off by Uncle no. 41."*

A smattering of applause followed. Uncle no. 41 was the well-known owner of many fast food restaurant chains.

Appeased by this reaction (finally!), Uncle no. 34 continued, "And most excitedly, a new fast-food-cum-coffee-cum-dessert-cafe chain will be launched. It will be called Brakefast Xpress."

"But will it work?" Finally a question from Uncle no. 19. He was bored of seeing someone else hog the remote control for so long. "Is it working?"

"Like a charm," Uncle no. 54 said with an oily smile. "It's so easy, distracting children. So important, distracting children, you know . . . because umm . . ." he fumbled, looking at Uncle no. 34.

"Because it's the children the tree talks to—well, some children. And then they incite other children to save the environment. And they become tree huggers. And shout 'Chipko' or something equally annoying or derivative. I mean, it's been years since the Chipko Andolan happened. Get off your high horse and find some new terms." He paused, realizing he was rambling and again, everyone had stopped listening to him.

"Yes, yes, absolutely," Uncle no. 54 said. He finally got up and opened his arms expansively. "Welcome to the Age of Distraction. I am so glad I thought of it."

Chapter 23

They Said.

The next day, I was dull and early at school, matching the dull weather of the day. With a nod to Pushpaji (and handing her a homemade granola bar), I went to the ground. I munched on my chocolate hazelnut granola bar and walked up to Tree and said, "Spill."

I touched the bark and . . .

They said:
    Trees?
    We don't talk
    or move.
    Don't feel pain.
    Do we?

Nice try, stop pulling a TLEU (ATA) on me. I was not going to get distracted by poetry anymore. I needed facts and I needed them now. I glared at Tree, and I could have sworn they gave me an exasperated swishing of leaves back, right alongside an orchestra of wasps. I couldn't tell if they sounded angry or happy—that was Gia's domain. At least I was now *almost* used to them— as long as they didn't come too close.

Yes, Tree—trees talk, move, feel pain. You are all awesome, I heart you all. So now tell me about Dad.

My phone pinged.

Toffee: We will pick u up, Savi? Breakfast at Brakefast Xpress—pancakes!
Mausam: And smoothie bowls.
Raina: SAVIIIIII?!

I realized I had not responded last night and had missed a truckload of messages about the show as well as tons of pictures of ramen in fancy bowls. *Yikes!* I quickly typed.

Me: Didn't finish Maharukh's HW ya. Full bore. Finishing now.
Toffee: :(Boo.

I switched my phone off, swung myself up, like Samar had, and to my delight, I was up on Tree. It wasn't that difficult once I knew what to do. I settled back, waiting.

But nothing. Except AN AUDIBLE CREAKING OF BRANCHES.

"Don't sigh!" I was not giving up this easily. "I skipped breakfast for this, and now I am feeling hangry, so come on. We are doing this." I didn't want to speak too loudly in case anyone else was around. "Earthworms, do your thing. Or fungi. Or whoever."

I could almost hear Tree thinking. It was time to tell me their stories. And finally, I felt myself slipping, surrendering to that earthy feeling covering me again.

I was right there, by Tree. For a minute I thought I was in present-day Shajarpur, but the air was much clearer—in fact, it was so clear it hurt my eyes. I blinked and realized that a very young Dad was there. My heart started racing. I saw a bunch of other children there too.

"Didn't you hear his surname?"

"My dad said they are one of those."

Another loamy smell. Same children, this time, they were hooting with laughter.

"It's pronounced kuh-nuhl, not colon-nel." A boy with incredibly wavy hair was laughing. All of the boys were in cricket uniforms.

"This is an English-medium school—learn English," another said. He was short, plump, and was red in the face with laughter.

"Remember when he said Mauritius in Geography. Hey Abhay, it is Maw-RISH-us. Not Mau-reet-eus."

"Come back when you know the rules of this game. It's also English, you know."

I wanted to shout that Dad spoke English, Hindi, Marathi, Konkani, Gujarati, and had taught himself French and Spanish. Dad kept walking, he didn't look back. Instead, he gripped his cricket bat harder. Suddenly, I remembered something. Dad had been the first in his family to get a formal education. Baba, his father, had been so proud, he always said.

Once again, I was surrounded by luminosity and the loamy smell. Now I was in a classroom. An almost balding teacher in a safari suit was pointing at a diagram of earth and its many atmospheric layers. He was talking about the atmosphere and the stratosphere. "Can you name the greenhouse gases?" he asked.

A number of hands went up. I noticed the same boys who had been bullying my dad were in the class. They were sitting at the back, passing notes, and flicking chalk at the front benchers, including Dad.

"Carbon, methane, and nitrous oxide," said one boy.

"*Correct*," *the teacher replied with a nod.* "*Now, who can tell me what they do?*"

The hands went down except for Dad's. The teacher sneered and said, "*The RTE student seems to know all the answers. Yes, Abhay?*"

Dad's face flushed, and I realized he was gritting his teeth. Just like me! "*Sir, they help regulate earth's temperature. But now there is too much carbon and methane in the atmosphere, causing global warming.*"

The teacher shook his head and said, "*Incorrect. Global warming is a hoax invented by tree huggers.*" *He turned to the board to label the diagram and muttered to himself,* "*Spoiling school culture with reservation. Good-for-nothings!*" *The classroom sniggered.*

In another space, a game of cricket was just over. Clearly, Dad's ragtag team had won, and everyone was high-fiving and hugging. "*Great catch,*" *one boy said. He turned to the rest of the team and yelled,* "*Naashta at my house!*" *Everyone cheered and strolled towards the gate. The boy turned to Dad and said,* "*Achchha, see you tomorrow at practice.*"

I couldn't believe it! Why did Dad love this city? This city full of people who bullied him, who made fun of him. It could not just be the climate. I wanted to yell at Mom for bringing us here, to the place where he had been so unhappy. But just then, I was swept back into the loamy, luminous feeling, and I was back on Tree, as was Dad. He was so close, I could have reached out and touched him.

"Dad," I whispered. I expected him to look angry, teeth-gritty, fist-clenchy. But he was scribbling in his notebook and talking aloud.

"So today, I spotted a two-tailed spider, it was pretty amazing. Perfectly camouflaged against the trunk of the tree. And just above her was a huntsman spider! Her web spanned two trees—must be some six feet apart. She was as big as my hand.

"Yes, yes, and guess what! The jacarandas are finally flowering. My lane's just a carpet of purple. I brought home some flowers for Baba—you know how much he loves them. Aai and he used to take long walks and he'd string them together. Only the fallen ones, though, he hates anyone plucking flowers. He misses Aai so much. So do I. But you know, yesterday we ordered in raniya rotis. I have to learn how to make them."

Your dad was such an Ent.

The memories swept over me like waves and, when I returned to the real world, my heart was hammering, my mind was racing. My father visited Tree, climbed their branches, and told them about the unkindness that he could not understand. Of his grandmother who died before his eyes because the hospital wouldn't treat her. Of his parents, the first generation of his family who worked in offices. Of their hopes for him, the first generation to study. Of his Aai, gone too soon.

Tree, in turn, told him their stories, of life and death, of the changing winds of time. Of looking towards science and nature to find answers—that trees gather together so that they can thrive as a community, that a dying tree gives its food and nutrients to its neighbors so that they can live. Of not being in a hurry to grow up—grow slowly, like a tree—tall and strong.

Dad was bullied, for his surname, for where he came from. Yet, with Tree, he found himself. It defined the work he did—working with students from marginalized communities, empowering them through education, offering them spaces to just be themselves. OH! All those Delhi Ridge walks he took his students on. It all made sense now.

No wonder he loved Shajarpur, though—it was where Tree lived. No wonder that Mom had brought us here. It was Dad's Narnia, a place where magical things happened; a place where he could be who he was, where he could talk about his grief over losing Aai . . . I had never thought that Dad also had lost a parent like us or about how he must have felt.

That was probably why, when he left Tree behind, he needed the solace of green things, the feel of soil under his fingers; the rich, earthy smell from the first rain; someone to talk to when he was angry with the world, when it was all too much for him. And they, like Tree, held his stories.

Now they had all come together to tell me his stories and their stories.

The school bell rang, and I remembered this messed-up, real world I lived in. Tree was SO not going down. I had an idea.

I heard some scuffle and looked down. The glowing, perfumed faces of the Very Cool and Hip People were peering at me. "That's your homework?" Raina mimed throwing up. "What is it with you and this tree? Are you becoming a tree hugger too? Come on, time for English!"

Chapter 24

Candies from a Baby

A seedling of a plan was growing in my mind. Of course, we needed to know what TLEU (ATA) was up to. Try as I might, Tree wouldn't tell me.

The Ents were after me constantly. "Did Tree say anything?"

"What's TLEU (ATA) up to now?"

"Evil, they're just pure evil."

"I am not some Wi-Fi router that I can just connect to their network, guys," I said, but they kept badgering me. I was scared to tell them that I suspected Tree was weakening. I was scared to even say that out loud.

So, for the last few days, every time during break, I would rush to Tree and hold them, telling the Very Cool and Hip People that I needed to go to the bathroom. At last, after spending an entire lunch break pleading with

Tree, I sunk into their memory, but this time around, it wasn't a boardroom.

"This is highly abnormal." Uncle no. 54 pushed his sweat-shirt sleeves up as he addressed TLEU (ATA). They were meeting at a jogger's park. "Look, I am telling you, our reports tell us that the kids are up to something."

"Listen, kids are stupid—their brains are not fully formed," Uncle no. 14 said. "That's why they go to school, to learn things. They're up to nothing good only. All they do is create mischief and break windows. The other day, this brat was playing cricket in the park and her ball came . . ."

"Wow, they still play cricket?" Aunty no. 2 said. "That too outside?"

"Are you sure it wasn't a USB stick or, you know, a console?" Uncle no. 65 asked.

"It was a ball—I recognize cricket balls," Uncle no. 14 said. "How do you chase after a console?"

Everyone in the park fell silent.

Uncle no. 14 cleared his throat. "So, where was I?"

"Your cricket ball."

"Not mine. That brat's. Anyway, that's not the point, is it? It's just that children should not be allowed to play in parks where people go for walks."

"I think we were talking about the tree actually."

"Yes, yes, I was getting to it. Stop interrupting me," he harrumphed. "Yes, the tree. Work starts in two weeks on felling the tree."

"Yes, but isn't it strange that there have been no protests, no noise on social media, nothing?" It was Uncle no. 34. He looked bewildered.

"Is it really? Who would dare? Who would also remember to . . . ?"

Everyone burst out laughing. Hooo hooo, haaaa haaaa, heeee heeee. They raised their hands and wriggled them in the air.

That was true. Over the last many years TLEU (ATA)'s nieces and nephews and their cousins had slowly taken over news companies, websites, and social media sites. They'd also taken over malls and media companies and ad agencies and publishing houses—all sound investments—which meant that now the only news and stories that got out were the ones they wanted out. Like how felling this tree was good for Progress. There were movies being made about this and a web series, even documentary films. Social media influencers were peddling this amazing story to their thousands and millions of followers.

"So what is the problem?" asked Aunty no. 1, who had dialed in via video call.

"*Those kids,*" Uncle no. 34 said. "*They are making no noise in the school. I get the feeling that something is afoot.*"

"*They've been distracted,*" Uncle no. 54 said rather smugly. "*Told you, it was like taking candies from a baby. Well done, us.*"

I came back to the real world with a jolt and rushed to the canteen. I was torn between immediately telling the Ents what I had heard and not raising the hackles of my other friends. Already Toffee was offering me a range of digestive supplements. The Very Cool and Hip People it was. The Ents could wait until after class. I did not want more fancy Gelusil being thrust in my face.

Chapter 25

Mission, Not Rendezvous

At the emergency Ents meeting after school, Rushad, Gia, and Sana were sitting across from Maharukh Sir, Amba Ma'am, and Pushpaji. The floor was strewn with chart paper, photocopied pages, markers and sketch pens, and lots of reference notebooks. *Huh.* Even Samar was there. He was a puzzle, that one. It was ridiculously cold now, and everyone was bundled in sweaters and scarves and woolen caps. Everyone looked like a mountain of sheep. Tree looked adorable, swathed in a brightly knit purple and pink wrap.

"So, petitions to school, to municipality, and to who else?"

"Yes, online and offline. Let's do a hashtag and a social media storm. Isn't Savi's sister some major social media presence?"

"Do we have time for a PIL?"

"What's a PIL, bro?"

"It's a public interest litigation—how can you not know? Do you not listen in civics class?"

"Shhh . . . Maharukh Sir is right here. He doesn't need to know."

"Aye, what if they chuck us out of school for suing the school? We all can't be like those American kids who sued the US government for causing climate change or something like that. My Ammi will kill me—like proper skewer."

"Uff, shut up. We will if we have to."

"What else, what else?"

"Let's tweet Greta Thunberg, she will have some idea."

"Now who is Greta?"

"*Yaar*, how do you know nothing?"

"None of these are going to work," I said.

"Ah Savi," Gia said. "Always the life of the party." She looked at her watch and scowled. A wasp buzzed towards her and she muttered, "Fine, fine! I will try to behave. Why won't it work? We have to do something, right?"

"Look, we don't have the time, they have made up their minds. And have you not noticed? Other trees keep being felled everywhere. The protests start and then people get distracted by something or the other, and it fizzles out. I told you those were TLEU (ATA)'s tactics. I am not saying this doesn't work, but this time, we have to try something different." I quickly told them about the latest updates and the alarming news of TLEU (ATA)'s nieces and nephews. Strangely, no one else looked surprised.

"Well, we always thought there'd be their spies," Maharukh Sir said. But before he could continue, Amba Ma'am spoke up.

"How can it not work? You are giving up before trying." She looked disappointed, especially with me. Oh no, a disappointment glare was coming my way. That was even worse somehow.

"I agree—there are so many precedents of trees and forests being saved. Our country has some really strong laws," Maharukh Sir said. He turned to Gia. "This is why civics is important." He smiled to soften his remark.

"Yes, I agree," I said. I shivered, but not just from the cold. "But I have an idea. And I think it might just work."

"Ooh, she has an idea," Gia said, sarcasm oozing from every word. The wasp buzzed again. "I said I will try, okay? But I didn't promise."

I sat down and blurted it out before I could change

my mind or let Gia scare me. When I finished, there was a long silence and then everyone began to ask me questions.

"Hold on, hold on! I don't know, all right? This is only an initial thought. We need to work together to fine-tune it."

"I think it's silly," Samar said. "I mean, yes, you are skilled and all at communicating with Tree and your house plants, but this sounds a bit outlandish to me."

Everyone began nodding, but Gia turned to Tree. A swarm of wasps rose in the air, buzzing. "Tree heart-woodedly approves of the idea," she said with a sigh. She shrugged and looked at everyone else. "Well, it seems Savi's plan is Plan A. So let us plan away."

***

After what felt like forever, the weekend arrived. There were many things that could go wrong. Samar had helpfully pointed each one of them out. Frankly, I had absolutely no clue how this was going to go down.

First, sneaking into school on the weekend.

Second, planting messages to the human world using my secret skill, which, let's face it, was not really a skill. It was just bizarro behavior.

Third, making an excuse to get out of the house because the rendezvous (ugh, not rendezvous but mission—mission sounded way better) was not only on the weekend but at night. Apparently, we were less likely to be seen and heard.

I looked at Dad's photo and his plants—our plants. I could do this. I had to. I touched the sword lily for strength, but I didn't linger enough to let a memory suffuse me. My phone pinged—it was time to head out. Anyway, Mom was busy cleaning the kitchen. It seemed her new children were the broom and the duster.

I missed her. Or at least, I missed what I remembered of her. I definitely did not miss this ghost of a mother, who stared at us blankly, cleaned like a vacuum cleaner on triple power, who kept making plans and forgetting about them, and who paced up and down the teeniest, tiniest of flats every night.

"I am off to Sana's," I said, peeping into the kitchen. I had packed a bag because after the mission, I was actually going there. I picked up my raincoat because it now looked like rain.

Mom turned and looked at me, puzzled. "Who is Sana? The one with the shiny hair?"

"No, that's Raina—you met her and her parents at

the mall. This is Sana, part of my eco club. We have a project due tomorrow, remember?"

"Uh-uh," came the response. "Text me her number? Do I need to speak to her parents?"

I wanted to yell back that she only had a father, but I didn't because, for once, Mom actually remembered to ask. I sent her Sana's contact card. Her father was an Ent alumni and so he was totally cool with our plan.

Because it was late, I took an auto, which dropped me outside the school. "Baby, *aapko pakka yeh time pe* school *jana hai?*" the driver asked.

"*Hum* camping *jaa rahe hain*," I said, crossing my fingers behind my back. It wasn't a lie—we *were* camping. Sort of.

Despite the streetlight, our brown school looked browner than usual. Suddenly, something hooted, and I jumped. It was all too quiet. But as I got used to the silence, I heard the orchestra of the cicadas and felt less scared.

Where was everyone? Even Pushpaji was not by the gate. I looked at my phone and realized I was late. I hadn't expected to have a concerned conversation with Mom!

The gate was slightly ajar, so I slipped in and headed towards the ground. The importance of what we were doing dawned on me once again and, for some reason, I was splat in the center of this! As I neared the ground, I saw silhouettes and exhaled. It was a moon-filled night, fewer stars now than the Shajarpurians were used to. But still a clear enough night. I could make out Rushad, Sana, Gia, and our teachers. Sana had a big bag of food next to her. How did she think anyone would eat at such a time?

"Late," Rushad said, shaking his head.

Before I could offer my excuses—"Sorry, sorry," Samar piped up from behind. "Traffic, you know."

"Really, at this time?"

"There's always traffic," I said quickly, thankful that Samar had shown up when he did. "Thanks to our wonderful climate. Well, now less-wonderful climate. How do we do this? I am not holding hands." I put my hands behind my back.

Everyone laughed and shook their heads.

Rushad looked at me and said, "You know what you have to do. We are just accessories, as Gia loves to say."

"No one is an accessory," Pushpaji shook her head. "We all need to be here to make this work. We have to think of our person." She smiled sadly again. I wanted to hug her. Who was I, wanting to hug people? I was surprising myself! Tree was making me soft.

We all moved to Tree and formed a triangle around

them. The wasps rose as if they had been waiting and began to dance.

"They wish you luck," Gia said quietly. "And they say everyone is counting on us."

"No pressure then," I said. Yikes, my voice came out like a squeak. I cleared my throat and broke away from the triangle, getting closer to Tree. The group reformed behind me. Nobody was going to hurt a single branch of Tree. Well, unless it was natural forces, cannot help that.

I put my hands on the trunk and closed my eyes.

Remember?

> *Remember when you were a child?*
> *And climbed your first tree?*
> *Smelled a rose for the first time?*
> *Ate your first mango?*
> *Heard a bird chirp outside the window?*
> *Stood in awe, as an elephant passed you in the forest?*
> *Saw the waves on the sand*
> *For the first time?*
> *That wonder. That sense of wonder.*
> *Remember?*
> *Remember?*
> *Your person.*

Now stardust and soil.
Remember who you were with them.
Your grief, your loss.
You, without your person
Your person, always with you
Remember?

I could feel the deep thrumming of Tree as the message raced through the Wood Wide Web network, through the earthworm holes, moving quickly from one tree to another.

If anyone had been looking at the school—which they were not because it was nighttime and the only people who could have were the neighbors, who were sick of the school because of all the noise that came from it during the daytime—they would have seen a faint glow emanating from Tree.

Tree was bathed in silvery green moonlight. The light shimmered and shot through Tree, it went into the ground, from where it entwined into their many-fingered roots and sinuously made its way across the city.

I reached into my memories.

Dad was taking us for a long, too long, walk in the rho-dodendron forest of Binsar. I was just a toddler, and I felt like we had been walking for ages. But then Dad hoisted me on his shoulders, and suddenly I was surrounded by a sky of red. "The trees are blushing, like someone put rouge on them," Meher had pointed out. Mom had laughed and pulled her closer, giving her a hug, her hands still, not itching to clean something. I touched one of the velvety crimson leaves, the sunlight was playing hide-and-seek on the forest floor which crunched beneath our feet, and I felt safe on Dad's broad shoulders. I spoke my first word then, the late bloomer that I was, as Meher loved to constantly remind me. "Leaf" (or rather, "veaf"). Just then the leaf beat its wings and fluttered away. It was an oak-leaf butterfly, perfectly camouflaged.

Remember?

I felt something stir, it wasn't just my memory anymore. It was everyone's—

Amba Ma'am cutting her sister's fringe secretly in their garden, giggling nervously, a Betty and Veronica *comic lying next to them.*

Samar cooking mock Maggi over a mock fire with his brother in a makeshift sheet tent on their balcony, surrounded by tons of plants.

Pushpaji on a tree swing with her baby.

A mother applying nail paint to a toddler's thumb. It was Rushad, gurgling happily under a banyan tree as his father held him tightly.

Gia plucking a jamun as her nanny held her up to the tree.

Ammi tucking a hibiscus in Sana's freshly oiled hair.

Maharukh Sir standing under Tree, laughing with his partner, eating peanuts from paper cones.

And with that, something else stirred.

It was something deep under the soil, somewhere in the deepest recess of the earth. Something that felt alive, suddenly invigorated, as if they had just been woken up. It was something primal, something who held earth's stories, the narratives of all beings. It was that someone who stays right at the edge of your memory, just out of reach, but almost there, almost at your fingertips. It opened up the stories it held and let them out, finally.

"It's done." I opened my eyes and stepped back with a jerk. I was trembling. Gia slipped her hand into mine and squeezed. "I could feel it," she said.

Everyone nodded. Nobody could speak yet, but they had all felt it.

"What was it, you think?" Sana asked.

"I haven't the faintest idea," I said. "But whatever it is, it's now out there."

"Take that, TLEU (ATA)," Rushad said, raising a fist in the air. A tiny green shoot popped up in response right next to Tree, and everyone whooped.

Our grove of teenagers and three adults slowly walked out of school. We looked around—everything seemed normal.

Chapter 26

The Dance Party

Sana's father opened the door. He had a long salt-and-pepper beard, long salt-and-pepper hair, and eyes that twinkled. He ushered us in.

"Come in—you are Savi?" He solemnly shook hands with me, making me feel very grown-up. Sana turned to a large portrait of a beautiful woman, touched it, and said quietly, "Hi, Ammi!"

"I have heard so much about you," her father said. "Are you two hungry?"

We both shook our heads, but his face creased into a smile.

"There are caramel brownies," he said. His voice dropped, "So tell me, did it work, Sana?"

Sana began talking as they both headed into the kitchen. I shoved my bag into a corner and looked around her home. It was bright and cheerful, with yellow lamps everywhere—and it was so spacious. There were comfortable-looking sofas and squishy armchairs, and lots of photos of Sana and her mother and father on the walls, and even more plants in the garden outside. Everywhere I looked, I sensed there was a keepsake of her Ammi. Like in my house, here, too, hung that thick, heavy feeling of someone being missed.

I stepped back into the garden, the way we had come, hoping Sana wouldn't mind. Hers was one of the bungalows right next to school, and I hadn't even realized she lived in such a posh locality. She never seemed to talk about that.

It was such a glorious garden—perfectly ramshackle, with trees and plants growing everywhere. A huge Dutchman's pipe had formed a canopy under the *badam* tree. Its purple-white flowers and basket-shaped seedpods felt festive. Tomato, spider and rocket plants, fennel, ferns, and crocuses ran riot everywhere, cucumber and *karela* vines looped around a mulberry shrub. A toad sat in the lily pond pot as little fishes darted about. Dad would have loved this place. And he'd be proud that I could recognize most of the plants! Heck, *I* was proud of myself.

I gravitated towards their *raat ki rani* plant, which spilled all over their gate, and I took a deep breath, reaching out to touch one. Immediately, I knew something was terribly wrong.

The spell, it
  Ricocheted
  Reverberated
  Reflected
  Resonated
  But . . .
  Something was very wrong.
  I held on and waited.

Uncle no. 97 was late. He stepped into a dark room where a shiny disco ball flashed diamond shards of light across the dance floor. He blinked in rapid succession and quickly pulled on his sunglasses.

Music pulsed through the room—Bollywood and pop numbers from the '80s. He smiled to see his friends from The League of Extraordinary Uncles (And Two Aunties) boogeying away. Everyone, except Uncle no. 34, who sat grumpily in a corner, chomping on a paneer tikka. Everyone was—
  Aha,
Dancing, dancing.
Auva, auva.
All hands up in the air.

Auva, auva.

All legs moving to the right.

Auva, auva.

All doing a naagin dance.

TLEU (ATA) were celebrating. Uncle no. 97 joined them quickly.

Bang, bang,

Trees were dying.

The darned tree's deathly day was close.

Bang, bang,

More buildings.

More flyovers.

More concrete.

Bang, bang.

"Statue," Uncle no. 35 announced, holding his hands up and striking a pose like Elvis.

Everyone immediately froze.

"No, no," he said, "not the game! I mean, we must build a statue. To commemorate our work."

Everyone unfroze and cheered. "Yes, more statues. More!"

Everyone raised their hands in the air and resumed dancing.

Tree knew their days were numbered.

They knew the tree's days were numbered.

It was definitely a gold-letter day.
Auva, auva.

"Savi?" Sana and her father were standing by their door, looking worried.

I shook my head. Tears ran down Sana's cheeks as her father enveloped her in a hug.

Chapter 27

Phuss Went the Plan

"HOW'S IT NOT WORKING? WE DID EVERY-THING. I COULD FEEL IT, OKAY? WHAT IS THIS NONSENSE?" Rushad paused mid-stride and began pacing again. "No one has changed. Nothing has changed. NOTHING AT ALL." His mood was shouty, and he pursed his lips so as not to shout anymore.

We understood how he felt, though. School was about to be shut for holidays and soon, our historic Tree would be relegated to history. Rushad mopped his forehead with a hanky. Today was so warm. Immediately, he sneezed. The constant change in weather was terrible for his allergies.

"You must have done something wrong, Savi," Samar finally said what everyone had been thinking. The mood was tense at the club, and both the teachers were huddled in a corner with Pushpaji whispering fervently.

"No!" I glared at him. He was supposed to be my friend. "I mean, I don't actually know what I was supposed to do. I just did what we thought would work. I mean, it was just an idea, and I also wasn't sure." I threw up my hands in the air and looked at them, pleading. "And Tree agreed to it."

"Well, it was supposed to make people remember that nature's awesome," Sana said.

"You know," Gia said. "Don't you think this was a bit of a lofty goal? Like 'Ooooh, look nature!' after years and years of 'Nature bad, concrete good.'"

"Or rather nature *kaun*," Rushad pointed out.

"Yes," Sana said, "but Tree agreed it would work— like going-back-to-our-roots types."

"Plus, maybe we misread what the wasps said," Samar offered. "Maybe it's not Savi." He didn't look at me and instead, he turned to Gia.

I suddenly felt a rush of relief, like someone had doused me with cold water on a hot, hot day. I nodded quickly, "Yes, that's it! Samar's right. Maybe it wasn't meant to be me. I mean, you know, I am just a random girl, and you all assumed it's me. You know what they say, the word 'assume' makes an ass of you and me! That's what it must be. Samar, you're a genius."

Samar stared at me. He looked surprised. Plus, I had called him a genius. He had clearly thought I would be furious at his suggestion, but I was positively thrilled. Maybe that ritual, or whatever they did, had addled my brains. Or maybe it was the heat causing it.

I was beaming at everyone and nodding. "It must be Gia, she can talk to the wasps. Or Rushad and Sana— they're presidents of the club or whatever designation they've tacked on to themselves. Or you know, even you, Samar, with your talent. That's why it didn't work, it wasn't me." I finally sat down on the ground, as if the air had been let out of me. "Or even the grown-ups," I quickly added, not wanting to leave anyone out, though I was pretty sure it was meant to be one of us teenagers.

"Now she's just reciting all our names," Rushad said with a grin.

But Gia was shaking her head. "No, the wasps are never wrong. How many times to tell you, Savi? They insisted it's you."

"Maybe it's not her," Samar said, gently. He knew Gia could get mad at the drop of a fig fruit.

But this time, to my utter surprise, Gia didn't get angry. Instead, she spoke softly, "The wasps said . . . I didn't tell you all everything." She picked up some soil and crushed it between her fingers, letting it fall back onto the ground. She suddenly looked all awkward. "I was jealous, okay! Until now, only I could communicate with Tree, and then she came along. But I got an earful from the wasps, and now I have dialed it down. Slightly."

A swarm of wasps surrounded Gia, as if to bolster her.

"The wasps—they knew it had to be Savitri." Gia turned her back to the club and me. It was like she was talking to herself and the wasps and no one else. I was so astonished that I didn't even correct her for calling me Savitri. "It's her because she is a child of this land. Her father—he was of this land. His, Savitri's—their ancestors are of this land."

I opened my mouth to speak, I couldn't believe that Tree had spilled my secrets! But Gia was talking like she was in a trance, the words spilling out of her in a gush. "They were the first dwellers here. They planted our Tree as a protector of their land, of their lives. Under Tree's canopies, generations lived and grew. They loved Tree, and Tree took care of them in return. But when the dominant ones came, they couldn't do anything as they were pushed out of their own land—forbidden from touching the pure water, from staying in the land that was theirs. That *is* theirs. They were pushed out, and pushed out, to the fringes, until they retreated. History was rewritten. But the land remembers, Tree remembers. You, Savi . . ." Gia finally turned and leaned against the tree, "are a child of this land."

Everyone who was listening to Gia turned to me. I could feel the blood rushing to my face and gulped.

"People, let's stop staring at her," Samar said, finally. "She's turned as red as a watermelon."

They all burst out laughing and that dispelled the tension in the air. I tried to smile my thanks at Samar, but all I managed was a weak chin wobble.

"Speaking of watermelon, I made some watermelon candies," Sana said, opening a freezer bag. "It's the only thing that works in this heat."

Everyone surrounded her, each taking a candy, except Rushad whose eyes were watery from his allergies. Sana held out one to me, but I got up and began walking away, first slowly, then quickly. But then . . . I turned and came stalking back.

I'm pretty sure I was still watermelon red, but I was now red with anger.

"Then. Why. Is. It. Not. Working?" I ground out, crossing my arms and addressing Tree.

A lone wasp started to rise from the canopy, but as she did, and before Gia could begin to translate, Sana put up her hand.

"You know you don't have to raise your hand right now, right?" Samar said, shaking his head. "You are not in class."

Sana quickly put her hand down and bit her lip nervously. "I think I know what's wrong."

The wasp paused, as if waiting, hovering over Tree.

"It's because no one cares," she said.

"Surprise, surprise," Rushad said.

"Tell us something new," Gia said.

"Wait, let's listen to her." I still had my arms crossed and was feeling so angry that I was glad no one wanted to interrupt me right now.

Sana took a deep breath and continued, "It's actually pretty simple. To remember nature, to go back to our roots, metaphorically and literally speaking, we need to be in touch with nature." She waggled her fingers to make the quote-unquote sign.

"And no one is actually engaging with nature," Amba Ma'am said. The grown-ups had arrived, probably about the time my face was turning a shade of fruit.

"Yes! It's like 'Eeeks, mud!' or 'Ughhh, caterpillar!' or 'Kill that spider!'" Rushad said. "Or build roads and cut forests and render elephants and leopards homeless and take land away from . . ."

"Or, you know, what was that, ah yes—yell like a

banshee when they see a biting wasp," Samar said, a sly grin plastered on his face. "Maybe we should rename it to 'yell like Savi!'"

"And this means people are staying away from nature. Literally not stopping to smell the roses or the *raat ki rani*," Sana ignored Samar and kept talking. "People have become like pigeons, preferring to roost in concrete over trees."

"Yes!" Gia nodded. "Exactly! How can you get enchanted by a spell if the spell doesn't touch you."

"You're a genius!" Rushad said, and he went to give Sana a hug. He stopped, remembering his allergies, and fist-bumped her instead.

The wasp buzzed. "Clocked on, have you?" Gia translated with a smirk. Everyone rolled their eyes and shook their heads at the cheeky wasp.

"But then, what should we do?" Samar asked.

Sana raised her eyebrows and said, "Isn't it obvious?"

Samar sighed and replied, "I wouldn't ask then, would I?"

"We get nature to engage with them," Sana said, a pale smile on her face, as she stepped towards Tree. "For that, all of us need to put our talents to use. Samar, you need to talk to the pollinators; Gia, you rally the wasps; Rushad, the plants have a job to do; and Savi, you need to send a slightly different message across. We need to do this together."

If I could smile, I would have. I settled for sending more blossoms flowering across the city. Red, yellow, purple, orange, pink, a blaze of colors. My roots connected with other roots which connected with other roots and, just like that, the city of Shajarpur began to remember.

I smiled, holding on to Tree.

The trees, the soil, the birds, and animals are a reminder of the world that was, of what it could be.
Our magic ricocheted around the city, drawing everyone into the spell.
My heartwood sang, even though I was still weary, my tree rings still gathered close.

Chapter 28

The Shajarpur Reclamation

The next day, the citizens of Shajarpur woke up to a regular morning.

It was a regular day by regular day standards.

Sun, check.

Smog and haze obscuring sun, check.

"Good morning, Shajarpur!" on the radio, check.

*Dabba*s being packed frantically, check.

Joggers running and not running, check.

But as they packed their *dabba*s, they felt something. As they jogged, they felt something.

As they listened to the radio and watched the day unfurl, they felt something.

A very strange something. I tuned into Tree Channel.

Shankar Bhai was cutting cucumbers for a sandwich order, snow-white bread slathered with chili-coriander chutney and salty butter, layers of thinly sliced cucumbers, boiled potatoes, tomatoes, and onions spread out in front of him, when he paused. The cucumber reminded him of his home-town, in the far corner of Bihar where, on his mother's farm, cucumbers grew alongside jute and sugarcane. He would pluck one and run up to the banyan tree by his house and eat it, skin and all. His customer clicked her tongue impatiently, and he was jolted back to the present, deftly beginning to slice the cucumbers into paper-thin coins.

Neema Mausi was preparing her daily thirty dabbas for office-goers, and as she pulped the tamarind, she smiled. Suddenly, she thought of the imli she'd plucked from the tree right outside her house in Chinchwadi as a child.

Imran Bhai was running to catch his train—he was going to miss the 8:26 a.m. if he didn't hurry—but then a mahogany seedpod came whirling from its tree and landed on his head. Exasperated, he reached up to brush it off. As his fingers touched the polished brown surface, he slowed down, thinking about how Seema and he used to throw these helicopter seedpods high up in the air and hold compe-titions to see whose winged seedpod would reach the ground last. Instead of throwing it down, he tossed the seedpod up in the air. Passersby couldn't help but stop and smile as they saw Imran Bhai laughing at the whirring blades, sunlight glinting off his glasses. His smile was so infectious that soon, some fifty people were tossing winged seedpods into the air and the air rang with laughter. That day, Imran Bhai missed his train for the first time in seventeen years, but he didn't mind. Not even when his boss gave him his famous "you are so in trouble" glare.

Reva was heading to Sumi's for a round of Clash Royale when she heard a rustle and looked up at the rain tree canopy above her. She ground to a halt as she saw the branches stretched above her, like an intricate lace table cloth. She stood there craning her neck, game date forgotten.

Aamir stared morosely at the apple in his lunch bag. After a meal of mutton rolls, this didn't quite cut it as dessert. He thought longingly of the chocobar in his office cafeteria but then his cook's angry face swam in front of his eyes. Sighing, he bit into the apple and before he knew it, he was transported back home, which was surrounded by apple trees, their aroma lingering in the air, enveloping him like a hug from his Ammi. The next day, Aamir's team was treated to homemade apple pie and cinnamon ice cream before their team meeting.

At the Chubby Cheeks, Dimpled Chin Nursery School, Radha Miss gave up trying to chase her toddler students as they ran after bright butterflies, giggling and stumbling. She smiled and felt her heart lift a bit, forgetting about the stack of medical bills at home for some time.

Sheila was furious—she was pacing her room up and down, left and right. "How dare they? How dare they?" kept playing in her mind on loop. To clear her head, she decided to go for a walk. She passed by an Arjuna tree and promptly tripped on a root. As she slammed to the ground, she spluttered and made to get up. She noticed an army of ants walking up and down the root. For the next hour, Sheila forgot her problems and watched the busy ants as they went about their day. When she got up and dusted her pantsuit, wincing at the pain in her toe, she wondered why she had been so angry.

Felita Ma'am was teaching nouns and pronouns when a purple sunbird flew into her classroom and hovered over her head as she yelled, "Help! It will do potty on me!" But the bird paused on top of the blackboard. As all of Class IV-F looked at the bird, mesmerized by its glossy purple feathers, the bird did a little pirouette and flew out of the room. All of Class IV-F got up and followed. There was no English class that day.

Ragini took a break from selling peanuts at the traffic signal by sheltering under the jamun tree. SPLAT! A jamun fell on her head and she turned to glare at the offending tree. The floor was stained with purple splotches from the fallen fruit already. She held up her hand to complain and a jamun fell on it. Her daughter, returning from school, grabbed it and gobbled it up. She beamed at her ma with her purple-juice-stained teeth and tongue, and Ragini's heart sang.

A group of municipality workers began cleaning up a floor of yellow copperpod flowers when suddenly the flowers whirled up, as if caught up in a tornado. Shanta, Jeev, and Mukund stopped and held each other's hands, watching this fiery blaze as it moved around them, gently touching their faces. Then, as if a wind had died down, the flowers fell back on the road.

Sonam and Aneesh decided not to go to Past Food Nation for a change. Instead, they went to the park and set their wailing toddler under the jacaranda tree. Before long, all three were lying on the purple blanket of jacaranda blossoms and making mud angels.

Ashish stomped out of the meeting, into the elevator, and straight to his office's terrace garden, where no one would see his tears of anger. He clenched his fists and was about to kick a pot when the smell of champas tickled his nose. He thought about his ma, who always put the white-and-yellow flower in her tightly braided plait, and his anger melted away as he took yet another deep breath. He squared his shoulders and returned to the meeting. He was going to get this. He just knew it.

At the most crowded Milk Road Junction, sealed,

*air-conditioned cars stretched out for miles, vendors weaved
in and out selling magazines and sliced sugarcane, and
people scurried to catch buses and find their cabs and autos.
All of them were busy staring at their phones, heads stooped,
shoulders hunched, eyes glazed. A flock of red-vented bul-
buls broke out into song, going on and on, getting louder, as
their numbers swelled. They threw back their crested heads,
puffed out their chests, and sang. It was a song so compel-
ling that, one by one, people looked up from their phones,
rolled down their windows, and stared at the canopies above
them. Some burst into tears, most put their phones aside,
and everyone stopped to listen. As the signal turned green
and the cars drove on, each person felt like they had left
someone special behind. It felt something like loss.*

*Slowly, it was as if nature was extending a hand or,
in some cases, putting out a root to trip people up to make
sure they opened their eyes.*

If I could, I'd have given Tree a high-five. But not
with those sharp branches. Instead, we settled for a hug.
Seriously, who was I turning into?

Chapter 29

Cushioning the Blow

It was working! Finally. Or at least it had to be. The proof was right in front of my eyes.

I beamed at our plants. They felt like my plants now, and not just Dad's. The spilling aloe vera, the heady-smelling mint, the lemon plant, the cacti—everything was bursting with life, as bees and butterflies and moths visited them. Not to mention the pigeons who tried to sit on them and squash them—even the cactus!

Everyone was flourishing. The climate was almost back to its regular, happy self. The people were suddenly la-la all over again (well, you can't win everything).

All except the jasmine plant. The stupid thing was still brown as a bug. Languisher. I frowned at Bekku, who was still using the jasmine pot as her favorite sleeping bag. But even the plant's obstinacy couldn't keep me down for long.

The wasps and Tree had reported success. People were finally getting in touch with nature, with their true selves, with the environment they lived in—not seeing it as something that was separate from them, but seeing themselves as part of it all.

Feeling lighter than I had in forever, I picked up Bekku and my school bag, and closed the door to my room to go to school. Meher had already left, as usual. Then what I saw made me stop in my tracks.

Mom was not cleaning! Her hands were still! She was sprawled on the sofa, hugging a cushion and sobbing.

I looked frantically at the door, wondering if I should just slink out. Maybe Mom wouldn't notice. These days she didn't seem to notice anything anyway. Not the late-night meetings that I had been attending, not Meher's obsession with her phone, nothing.

I began to move towards the door, when I saw the cushion Mom was hugging. It looked familiar.

Oh!

The purple frog on my heart pressed down a bit harder. It was a cushion cover made out of my father's second favorite shirt—bottle green with dark green checks.

Mom looked up, tears streaking down her cheeks, blurring her glasses. "Baba had it made," she said. "It just . . . just arrived." Baba now lived in Almora, surrounded by forests and valleys. We had only seen him once since Dad's death, at the funeral, so this was a surprise. It struck me now that he must miss his son. Just like each of us had retreated onto our own grief planet, so had he. We needed to visit him ASAP, I realized. Death, it complicates relationships.

Bekku wriggled out of my arms, ran towards Mom, and jumped lightly onto her lap. The cat stayed away from the cushion, as if she knew she couldn't shed on it. She purred, her green eyes staring at me accusingly, as if she knew I was going to do a runner on them.

What sort of a lowlife did Bekku think I was? A year earlier, I would have just pretended not to have seen this and slunk out. But now I was someone who hugged trees. I dumped my school bag and sat down on the arm of the sofa, next to Mom. I tentatively reached out. I wanted to . . . oh, I touched the cushion, feeling the soft, worn fabric. I tried to blink back tears, but now they wouldn't stop.

Mom moved her hand and put it on top of mine and squeezed it tight. It was as if the purple frog had finally slid off my heart. I moved next to her and hugged her tight. It felt like everything I had been holding in, every thought, feeling, emotion, was pouring out of me with my tears. Bekku licked our entwined hands, her whiskers brushing our arms lightly.

We sat like that forever. Finally, Mom's phone pinged. Usually her first reaction was to reach for it and forget everything around her, but today she just ignored it. Something shifted in me, and I said, "Mom . . ."

Mom shook her head and gripped my hand tighter, almost as if she was holding on to it for life. "I am so sorry, Savi, so, so sorry," she finally said. "I've been a terrible mother . . ."

I wanted to protest, to deny it, but I just couldn't find the words. It was true, our mother had been in another world, wrapped up in her grief, so intense and private that she hadn't been able to let either of us in—especially me. At least Meher had seemed to be able to talk to her. I had no words. But for now, I didn't need them. I squeezed her hand back.

"I have. Don't shake your head. You lost your father too. And it's not fair you had to lose your mom. It was all just too much, you know—the insurance, the provident fund, changing joint accounts to single ones, and on top of that—just missing him so much. So fuc . . . very much." She let go of my hand after another squeeze and reached for the box of tissues. We had a box of tissues in every room, though I had switched to hankies because wasting this much paper was highly unnecessary. I made a mental note to buy hankies for everyone at home as well.

Mom said, "I am here now. Really." I realized that it wasn't just her. I had spent so much time thinking about Dad, that I stopped thinking about Mom.

Just then, Meher came barging in. "Savi! You didn't make it to the school bus. I had to come back all the way for you. I am going to miss first period, thanks to you."

She stopped as she saw Bekku, Mom, and me sitting next to each other, tears, snot, and all. Why was crying so exhausting?

"Savi, what did you do?" she glared.

"Nothing," Mom said, holding out her hand to Meher. "She did nothing. Come here."

Confused, Meher took Mom's other hand and sat down on the floor. She looked from Mom to me to Bekku to the cushion, biting her lip.

Just like that Mom began talking, all the while holding on to Bekku, stroking her. And she wouldn't stop. It was like Gia when she went into that trance.

Mom talked about her depression, the fugue that she had been living in, that she inhabited even now. It had solidified inside her like *makhan* in the fridge. She hadn't been able to do anything, she'd just been buried in paperwork, and she had thrown herself into her work and, well, cleaning (she looked sheepish at this point)— so that she wouldn't remember, so that she wouldn't have to think. All she needed to do was just put one foot in front of the other. She told us how, in her grief, she had isolated herself, forgetting that not only had she lost her husband, but we had lost our father.

"But the other day," she looked at me, "Bekku kept running into your room, and I had to take her to the vet. She just wouldn't listen. So I followed her to catch her, and that's when I saw them . . . the plants. Oh Savi, you magician. Abhay would be so proud."

Mom didn't tell us that when she had chased Bekku into the room, the sight of the plants had made her stop and all thoughts of the doctor's appointment had left her. She had started crying and had not stopped until the smell of the jasmine had overpowered her, making her feel less alone. But it mingled with the sharp smell of mint, almost like a wake-up call, reminding her of her responsibilities. Of the grief not being hers alone.

It was too silly to put into words, what had happened in the room, Mom decided, so she left that bit out.

What she didn't know was that the traitorous jasmine

plant had spilled the beans to me. Well, traitorous to her, but fully loyal to me. I flushed and looked at the cushion. I was also pleased with my success with the plants, but more so that Mom had finally noticed. It was like she was waking up from a deep sleep punctuated with bouts of crying and long, heavy silences that weighed down our tiny apartment. And lots and lots of squeaky cleanliness.

"Does this mean you are not going to clean every godforsaken surface?" Meher asked. She was still looking confused, but I fully appreciated her asking this. The nation of this house needed to know.

Mom spluttered and shook her head. "Not all."

"Mom!"

"We'll see, we'll see. But we're all skipping today," Mom said, a watery smile on her face. "What say, we watch movies and eat pao bhaji?"

"With extra *makhan*," I said, with a grin. "And masala pao!"

Meher was so startled by the whole thing—our mother talking more than she had in forever, her sulky sister smiling sunnily—that, for once, she just nodded and didn't complain about the enormous amount of butter in the bhaji and pao. Or make a reel of the moment—though who knew how long she would resist?

"I'll get my phone and you can call school and tell them we're unwell!" I said. I jumped up and ran to open the door to my room. The smell of jasmine assailed me—the plant had burst into bloom. Pearl-white flowers studded the bright green plant.

For a minute, I considered not telling anyone, wanting to hug the secret close to me (see, more hugging!). After all, it was my plant. The plant shuddered visibly. I rolled my eyes and thought, fiiiine. "Mom, Meher, you won't believe it. Come here *right now!*"

Chapter 30

This So Wasn't Happening

Things were really looking up. The Shajarpur reclamation was well underway. The people were again looking shiny and happy (sigh, I did prefer that to droopiness), and they were all truly la-la over nature and trees and all things green. TLEU (ATA) was going to be outsmarted. The Ents were busy with their families and cousins over the holidays and so, apart from generic plant updates and news about the Shajarpurian reclamation, we weren't really chatting. Anyway, school was to start the next day, with yucky tests, but at least it meant that I could go and meet Tree every day. I missed them, just like I missed Dad. It was a slow, treacly missing.

Best of all, Mom had reduced cleaning by 42 percent, which really was an achievement. It meant I could finish my hot chocolate without it being tossed into the sink while it was still half full because I'd stepped away from it for 1/1,948,766th of a second. Bekku was relieved at not being followed by a lint roller, and Meher had reduced her reel-making habits. Turns out, I was right. She confided that she had resorted to stress dancing because she also had felt miserable at home. Well, if she had talked to me, we could have been miserable together. It loves company, after all.

Also, Dad's insurance money had finally come through, which had hugely improved Mom's mood.

I stuffed a pair of shorts and a T-shirt into my bag and tossed in my maths textbook. There were plans to go over to Raina's for a sleepover—she had promised a do-over with ramen. But it wasn't movie night. We were planning an all-nighter for the algebra test the next day. I needed the help because I sucked at algebra, and Mom had made it clear there wasn't enough money for tuition. "Why do I send you to a fancy school then?" she had complained.

I didn't trust Meher to water the plants, even though she had solemnly promised to. So I filled up a bucket and went around the house, giving them all a drink. I touched the jasmine plant, who was still all pearly white and happy green before giving Bekku a scratch behind the ears. That's when it happened. On came the lights and the loamy smell percolated through me, taking me back into that boardroom.

TLEU (ATA) were holding an emergency meeting and puja rolled into one in some maidan. As a bare-chested priest chanted mantras at top speed, tossing ghee into the fire in front of him, everyone's prayers rang up in the air.

Amidst the chants and the smoke and the dazzling array of shiny clothes and bling jewelry that would put Bappi Lahiri to shame, only snatches of conversation could be heard.

"The tree's no longer weakening."

"But the felling's still on track."

"Then why are we having this meeting?"

"Because everyone is now singing praises of nature."

"It is true. You know how everyone is dancing around trees in those Bollywood films? Now everyone is doing that in real life. It's as if some sickly love for nature spread and spread until it became thicker than the smog over Delhi. Che, che, che."

A collective shudder went around the room.

"Every time a tree is to be cut . . ."

"What?"

"The people they . . ."

"Start singing and dancing about it."

"Like proper music and all."

"I mean, some of them can't really dance."

"Yeah, it's a bit embarrassing."

"As if you can dance."

"I will have you know that my society voted me 'Saawan Khan of the Year.' And I dance better than you."

"Stop talking nonsense—all of you. So what, though? It's only some singing and dancing," said Aunty no. 2.

"I don't know," Uncle no. 34 said, hesitantly. "It is kind of nice, so much happiness in the city. Everyone dancing. And the weather's excellent. My grandchild was so happy the other day that we even went on a picnic."

Aunty no. 2 looked like she agreed with him, but she didn't say anything, but just gave a half-nod, half-shrug.

"Esh, they are total traas," another uncle said, dismissing him. "Who goes on picnics nowadays? So many keeda-makoras on the pakoras."

"Arre, chhe, chhe, it's like this proper blockbuster-type scene, with thousands of people—you can't even get the workmen close. And if you do, they drop their tools and start singing and dancing with them."

"You better not pay them."

"Have to—union rules, they showed up for the job, na."

"Asho, these union people I tell you. Pain in the backside only."

"*Okay, so you wait until they get tired and go home.*"

"*You think we didn't? Of course we did.*" *The voice muttered something about that particular uncle never having faith in them and how whatever he did was never enough.*

"*Then? Why are those trees still standing?*"

"*Because this city's got so much population that every time one crowd leaves, another just happens to be passing by. Even at 3 a.m. in the morning! I mean, it's either milk delivery boys and paowallahs, or its party-goers from, you know, debauched parties, or it's people finishing night shifts. Once, a whole group of cab drivers drove their cars in a dizzying circle and danced with their radios blaring loudly.*"

"*It is ekdum nonsense only.*"

"*We must ban dancing! And music.*"

"*We can't. It's part of our culture.*"

"*True, true. Culture's most important.*"

"*But this is not proper culture.*"

"*Oh, there have been groups of devotional music and dancers too—at 6 a.m. So really, banning them all might become a problem.*"

"*So now? We can't just sit one hand on top of the other, no?*"

"*Why are we sitting around? We're doing this havan for that only. Enlightenment will come.*"

"*Oh it has. It is time to place a call to our nieces and nephews. I have been missing them.*"

"No, wait. I will tell you."

Uncle no. 34 sighed. He almost knew what was coming next.

"It is time"—of course it was Uncle no. 54—"to call our nephews and nieces."

A cheer rang through TLEU (ATA).

"I'm so glad I thought of it," Uncle no. 54 said, pressing the stray white hairs on his forehead down. "Such a good plan it is."

Uncle no. 34 grimaced and shook his head.

Through the smoke, Uncle no. 54's smile glimmered like a certain maama in a certain epic. It looked like he was going to turn and pinch a child's cheek.

Chapter 31

The Algebra Test Prep

I had spent the last eight minutes pacing around the room, thinking about what I had seen and heard. Just when I decided to message the Ents, a horn sounded outside. I slipped the phone into my pocket. I was seeing them tomorrow, no point freaking them out tonight. Anyway, Raina's driver was already here.

I zipped up my rucksack, swung it on my shoulder, and stopped. A feeling of déjà vu descended on me—it felt like the same night that I had worked with Tree to send out, not exactly magic, but messages across the city.

Bekku rubbed her head against my ankles, entwining her body between my feet, making me almost trip. "Oh, stop it Bekku, not now," I said sternly. Usually Bekku ran away if she was scolded. But this time, she wouldn't stop weaving through my feet. I picked her up and plonked her on Meher's lap, who shouted, "Hey, I just put a typo on my post, thanks a lot!" I just grinned and, after hugging Mom, ran down. I could hear Bekku hissing behind me.

In the parking lot stood Raina's Hummer. Not her dad's, not her mum's, but hers. The tinted window of the passenger seat was down, and Raina was squinting up at our building. Kulkarni Uncle and Das Uncle were returning from somewhere, and they smelled of ghee. Kulkarni Uncle cleared his throat, so I muttered a greeting and ran to the car.

Raina rearranged her face and beamed, yelling, "In here." The passenger door swung open. Oh, Badal, Mausam, Toffee—everyone was there. Everyone except Samar. Raina had made it seem like it would just be the two of us, and I squirmed because I didn't know how Mom would feel about having guys at a sleepover. Badal was sitting at the back, while I slid in next to Mausam and Toffee.

I smiled nervously at the Very Cool and Hip People and, at the same time, my brain delivered a solid mental kick for still calling my friends that. It felt like years since I had seen them, even though it had just been days. But the event with Tree felt like it over-elmed everything for me.

The car started smoothly. Raina turned and chirped. "So who's all mugged up and ready?" she asked, her voice sounding extra cheery, but none of the others said anything.

Okay, definitely strange. Usually, they were chatting louder than the pigeons outside my window. Maybe everyone was nervous about the upcoming test, which was bizarre because all of them went to Balaram's Top Tuitions, whose poster "guaranteed cent percent results." Everyone went, except me, that is. *Thanks, Mom.*

As one, they all pulled out their phones and got busy on them.

I gave myself a mental shrug and looked out instead. "Umm, aren't we going to yours, Raina?"

"We are," Raina said, turning back again. "We'll take a small detour first. You don't mind, do you?" She beamed at me, but somehow that didn't make me feel better. I really needed to study. But I nodded and wondered if I should just go back home. This was all just too weird. And let's face it, I had had enough weirdness to last me a lifetime.

But almost as if the Very Cool and Hip People had read my mind, they put their phones away and began talking.

"Did you see that *Yeh Lo G*? Eww, what was she wearing on it?"

"And that makeup?"

"Dad said, you know, they live in a plastic world," Badal said, with a snigger.

"Bro, what a match yesterday."

"It was intense."

I looked at Mausam and Toffee, who beamed back at me, exactly like Raina.

Just then the car stopped. We were outside school.

Raina and Badal got out together in a manner that looked almost coordinated. Badal opened the door and mimed a bow. "Miladies, please step out of your not-so-humble carriage," he said, smoothly. "You can leave your bag. It'll just take five minutes."

I wanted to ask what we were doing back at school at night, but my voice had decided to stop working. I tried to say something but only a squeak came out, which I quickly disguised with a cough. I looked for Pushpaji, or for any of the other guards on duty, but the gate was open and unguarded.

"Pushpa's had an emergency back home," Toffee said. He sounded mournful. "Really unfortunate. Her remaining child, so very sad . . . we can only pray."

I couldn't believe it. Oh no, I needed to call her.

"The Ents didn't tell you?" Mausam asked, pulling a sad face.

Why hadn't the Ents told me about this? After all that we had been through . . .

But a hand gripped my arm, and I actually jumped. "Relax," Raina said. "So jumpy you are. It's not like this is the first time you've snuck into school at this time, is it?" She was still smiling, but suddenly she didn't look so pretty. Instead, her skin looked waxen, and her hair cloudy like the dark, moonless smog-filled night it was.

My stomach plummeted as I realized that we were walking towards Tree. Did they know? If so, would they laugh at me? Sneer at me? Oh no, was this going to be some weird ritual like in those American schools to initiate you into some other club. Just great—first the Ents' triangular ritual and now this.

As we neared Tree, I saw someone standing there. Please, please, please be an adult. I would have crossed my fingers but now Mausam was gripping my other hand. Why, I wondered, a hysteric giggle building up inside me right alongside the blossoming panic, did they always feel the need to flank me?

It was Samar. My knees almost buckled with relief. I waited for him to acknowledge me, but he was looking at Raina, a big smile stretched across his face.

"So, what do we have here?" he said, slowly turning

towards me. His eyes were dark, and I suddenly felt another clutch of fear. What the hell was happening? I knew Samar was part of this gang, just like me, but he was also a member of the Eco Ents. So why hadn't he given me a heads-up or something?

"So dramatic," sighed Badal. "You sound like a Bollywood baddie with that dialogue. Shut it, *yaar*—let's get on with it."

Samar didn't laugh but he fist-bumped Badal.

At the same time, Raina and Mausam relinquished their tight grip on my arms and moved away. I rubbed my sore arms; those two were surprisingly strong. I looked around and realized that the six of them had formed a circle around me.

"Ha, ha, very funny, guys," I said, finding my voice just in time. "Let's finish this prank and go home, shall we? I really need to study."

I tried to step away, but Toffee came and stood in front of me, still beaming.

"Not just yet, Savitri," Badal snarled. I turned to correct him, but the word "menacing" popped into my head. "Tell us, how did you do it?"

"Do what? Not ace algebra?" I asked, defiantly. When in doubt, be defiant, I decided. "Well, you all tell me. Maybe it's because I am standing here with you morons when I should be mugging up theorems and what-nots. Also, it's Savi."

"You know perfectly well what we're talking about, Savitri," barked Raina, stepping in front of me. The eerie beaming smile had finally left her face only to be replaced with a grimace. "Tell us NOW!"

Raina screamed and suddenly, I felt the air around us turn warmer—just like it had over the last few months.

"What are you doing? I . . . I . . ." my voice vanished, swallowed by the purple frog.

"I . . . I . . ." Badal mimicked me, and very poorly too. "You, yes, you. You tell us what you are doing. Why has the climate stopped changing? Why are the trees no longer weakening? Why?"

"Samar," I turned to him, but he shrugged.

His icy betrayal surged through me—he was supposed to be a friend. I had shared my secrets with him. He knew about the plants, my dad. He had told me about his brother, the hornbill's mate. And now he was here, turning on me.

"He can't tell us anything," Badal said, his handkerchief twirling in his hands. "He doesn't know anything; the tree doesn't talk to him. Useless he is. But you . . . it talks to you, so you can tell us."

"Tell you what?"

Just then Raina's phone beeped. "It's the uncles and aunties," I heard her whisper to Mausam. "They want to know the status. We're running out of time."

That's when I got it. I had finally met the "nieces and nephews."

Mausam turned to me and said softly, "Now, tell us, Savitri."

"I have literally nothing to tell you," I said, refusing to look at any of them. Instead, I looked at my last remaining friend—Tree. *Come on, you're my last hope.*

I cussed under my breath as not even one wasp buzzed.

Chapter 32

Just One Measly Sign. No?

Just one sign.

One. Something.

Dad?

Tree?

Wasps?

Really?

Nothing?

Not even a crummy fruit?

Or the smell of jasmine?

Fine, abandon me, just like Dad did.

As the thought flitted into my mind, I felt myself slump. My usually slouched shoulders curved even more. It was sheer willpower that my legs hadn't buckled. I wasn't going to crumple in front of them.

I peeled my eyes from Tree and looked at the People.

How had I ever thought they were cool, or hip, or even beautiful? They all now looked—not beastlike because creatures had beauty—unreal. They were straight out of the corners of the darkest imaginations of the worst minds.

"All right, I will tell you," I said, slowly. I needed to stall for time until some idea or some help came to me.

Raina smiled triumphantly, a diagonal slit across her face. Samar looked startled for a second, but his face became impassive again.

"But I need to go to Tree, to touch them, to tell you."

"Don't listen to her," Badal said. "It's got to be a trick. They warned us about her."

But Raina shook her head. "What's that old tree gonna do? Whip us with a root? Can't you see it's still dying?"

Everyone cackled as Badal flushed. The circle parted, as if their thoughts were connected with each other.

It took all the strength I had to walk slowly towards Tree. I didn't look at anyone, just straight at Tree. It felt like forever, but I finally reached them. Immediately, I felt suffused with strength, as if I was sitting by Dad. All wasn't lost, and I felt a surge of hope, which was immediately followed by the thought that this was such a grandiose statement. I took a shaky breath and went to touch Tree, hoping they would show me a memory. Something, anything. Some way out of this ambush.

I closed my eyes.

The League of Extraordinary Uncles (no aunties in sight) were in a huge auditorium. Five of them were sitting on the stage, behind a table bedecked with a stained white satin cloth, fringed with maroon curtains. Each one was wearing a big satin badge, denoting their status as VIPs. Names were called out by a master of ceremonies from behind a podium on the right side of the stage. Tweenagers, teenagers, and young adults came up on the stage and received a pat on the back from the uncles.

It felt like an initiation of some sort. Behind them a big banner read, "Progress: Our Great Nephews and Nieces. They Are Our Eyes and Ears."

Suddenly, it all made sense to me. An army of young people being greenwashed into believing that the only way to have a shiny future is for it to be one bereft of trees, of magic, of animals, of wasps, of fungi, of beings that weren't like them. By being made to forget that we were just a small part of this world. All for Progress's Sake. In the debate between economy and environment, for them, it was always only the economy. After all, money made the world go 'round, or at least *their* world.

For the rest of us, the earth continued to spin, with its glaciers and deserts, forests, and reefs.

UGH. My mind needed to stop wandering.

Tree hadn't shown me what to do next. What was I supposed to do with this knowledge? Wield it? Easier said than done. It wasn't exactly a sword. Now would have been a great moment for Tree to send me a fruit that magically turned into a weapon. Come on! Do a Percy Jackson and Chiron on me, I begged.

That's when I realized that even the nephews and nieces did not have any weapons. I opened my eyes slowly and turned to them.

"Well?" Mausam asked impatiently.

I didn't quite know what to do. But just then, I heard a yell, "Wasps, now would be great!"

As if they had been waiting for a command, a swarm of wasps descended from Tree, not just from our Tree, but from the neighboring trees as well, and formed a protective bubble around me.

My mouth fell open, and I closed it hastily because I did not want to swallow a stinging friend. All the Very Cool and Hip People began shaking and shimmering. Were they dancing, like their uncles and aunties? Were they okay?

I watched in horror as my once-upon-a-time friends

began sprouting feathers, their necks began to turn blue as if someone was choking them, their fancy sneakers turned into claws and their perfect noses elongated into beaks. In front of my eyes they turned into . . .

Pigeons. Giant rock pigeons. The ones we saw outside all our houses and, if they could find a way in, we'd see them inside too. The ones that were found everywhere—on windowsills and building tops, on parapets and balconies, on bathroom windows and in any holes, anywhere except trees. Those pooping, cooing pigeons. Only, each one of these was some seven feet in height and three feet broad. Their blue necks shone in the night, like radioactive beings, and their neon orange eyes stared blankly at me.

Honestly, if I had not been glued to the spot in fear, I might have burst out laughing. But they were terrifying. I felt grateful that I was protected from them by a wall of wasps.

The pigeons stood there for a heartbeat, and then they flapped their wings. I winced, but they didn't fly. Instead, they began to hop towards me. Just like the pigeons in my building. No matter how much anyone ran towards them, they just chilled in their spots, hopping a few inches away.

I stepped back instinctively. That's when I realized

Samar had not transformed into a pigeon. He was still 100 percent human. At least, I hoped so, unless this was another trick of his. He stepped behind the wasp wall and said, "What's up, Savi?"

Really? *Really? What's up?* I wanted to give him one tight slap. Instead, I looked at the pigeons, they were now bobbing their heads up and down most excitedly. Winged rats, someone had once called them. And it was not as if Samar was any less of a rat. Why was he not a pigeon?

Just then the plague of pigeons moved in, as if to attack us, and the wasps advanced. They weaved and danced and turned into a giant crested serpent eagle. As one, they charged at the pigeons. I winced, expecting a loud crash which, of course, never came. Instead, the pigeons and the wasps began a deadly duel. The pigeons advanced, the wasps receded. The wasps advanced, buzzing angrily, and finally attacked the birds, stinging wherever they could find feathers.

I cried out as some wasps fell, but more joined their ranks, keeping the serpent eagle formation intact. The pigeons tried to peck them, sit on them, fly around them, poop on them, but nothing worked. Samar moved closer to me, I wanted to step away, but I was still glued to the spot. I couldn't bring myself to look at him.

"Savi," he whispered. "You've got to believe me, I am on your side."

I kept staring at the fight in front of me, one that was all my fault. I had come here—why hadn't I fought them or called the cops? Or just run away? Why had I thought cool and hip people would want to befriend someone like me? The purple frog on my heart pressed down even more as a shower of wasps rained down, squirming, gasping, dying. I wanted to gather each one in my arms and hold them tight, keep them safe. Tears rolled down my cheeks. I couldn't bear it—not again.

I felt Samar put his hand over my shoulder. That's when I realized it was him who had yelled and summoned the wasps. I was almost as angry at him for pushing the wasps into battle. It was his fault as well. But then, surprisingly, he leaned into me. I didn't shake him off, and I *really* deserved a cookie for that. Where was Sana when you needed her? I realized I missed the Ents desperately.

"I am sorry," he said softly. I realized he wasn't talking to me, but to Tree and the carpet of dying wasps in front of us.

Then some things happened very fast.

A silvery green light emanated from Tree, just like that other night. The number of wasps doubled. A sound echoed from Tree. It was a keening sound, like an angry wail. It should have scared me, but it didn't, because I knew it wasn't for me. Or Samar. It wasn't meant to harm us.

The wail echoed around the ground. The pigeons froze. Then, they exploded into a debris of feathers, beaks, and claws, leaving a poop-and-wasp-encrusted ground behind.

The sound stopped immediately. The light disappeared, like someone had turned a switch off.

Chapter 33

The Traitor

I skipped school the next day. Of course, I would flunk my algebra test. But I still skipped. Anyway, it wasn't like I was prepared for the test. Then, I skipped the day after that. And the day after that. And the day after that. Then the weekend arrived. And I still couldn't bring myself to answer any of the Eco Ents' calls and messages. Especially Samar's.

I told Mom I was feeling ill, and I must have looked it because she let me be. She just sent an endless supply of soups, grilled cheese sandwiches, and *khichdi* my way, and no one else was allowed to hog Bekku.

It was easier to sit at home and pretend that I had not just narrowly avoided becoming pigeon feed, and stick with our plants, Mom, and my sister.

Finally, after five days, I picked up my phone. I scrolled to the Very Cool and Hip People's messaging group. It had . . . umm . . . vanished. I went and looked at their numbers on my contacts list—gone.

I pushed my phone away and decided to file it under the "Not My Problem" section of my brain.

I had other problems. Ever since our pao bhaji night, Mom seemed to have had a personality transplant, which was great, except she kept wanting to cook. And neither Meher nor I had the heart to tell her to, well . . . not cook.

So far, we had braved our way through *gobhi mush-wala*, watergate stir-fry, paneer so-not-*makhani*, and chocolate pudding with crispy burnt bits. Even Bekku had stopped popping into the kitchen looking for scraps.

Now we were sitting in the living room. I was pretending to read, and Meher was on her phone, when Mom said the dreaded five words again.

"What shall I make today?" she beamed, shoving aside her laptop.

Meher turned to me, eyes wide, with a pleading look. "Do something, do something," she was clearly signaling.

"Pizza," I said firmly. "You need a break, you're on *chhutti* too." Meher's expression relaxed as she nodded fervently.

"YES! Margherita."

"Uff, you're so boring," Mom said. "I saw they had one with paneer tikka."

"EWWWW, no," yelled Meher, just as the doorbell rang. "Next you'll want one with pineapples or even worse, tandoori peas or something."

Since neither of them had moved a toenail, I got up to open the door. Hopefully it wasn't any of the uncles, especially Kulkarni Uncle. I hated that suffix now.

Served me right for not looking through the peephole or not living in a society where they had fancy apps that announced who was coming in. It was Sana, Rushad, Gia. And Samar. And a wasp, perched on Gia's collar like a brooch.

Mom popped up behind me and beamed, "It'll be a pizza party! Come on in. Raina, Badal, Toffee, Mausam, right?"

My eyes widened and I quickly amended the introductions. I swallowed a scowl as the Eco Ents trooped in and sat down. Samar gave me a tentative smile, and instantly my scowl resurfaced. The nerve. Really.

My frown deepened as I saw Bekku jump into Samar's lap. Traitor. Worse, Bekku started purring with her eyes half-closed as Samar rubbed her head. Clearly, his talent extended to felines.

"What's his name?" Gia asked finally, after Mom and Meher promised food and drinks and disappeared into the kitchen. This had been followed by a long silence during which I refused to look at any of the members of my club. Instead, I stared at a damp spot on the wall. It was shaped like a butterfly. Fascinating.

"Her," I said.

"Sorry, sorry!" Gia giggled nervously.

"Her name is Bekku," I said.

Samar snorted.

"Funny, huh?" I snapped.

Samar's face immediately fell, and he said, "It's the name."

"Now my cat's funny to you all?"

"No, no," Samar said hurriedly. "It's just that in Kannada, *bekku* means cat."

"Wait, so your cat's called Cat?" asked Rushad. He looked so shocked that everyone burst out laughing. I reluctantly nodded.

The tension melted like the ice in the polar caps in our climate-changed world.

"She kind of adopted us," I said, "and we didn't get to name her." I looked around me and realized that everyone looked exhausted—just like how I felt—as if they had not slept for many, many nights. Or days. And they had spent those waking hours thinking and overthinking until their thoughts had become one big, tangled piece of wool that Bekku would have loved to have played with.

Just then the pizzas arrived, and chaos ensued as everyone chose their toppings, and glasses of iced mulberry milkshakes were passed around. Meher whispered to me that she had whipped them up and they were perfectly drinkable.

Mom and Meher once again made themselves scarce, their plates heaped with slices of pizza, smiles plastered on their faces. For a minute, I wished I could go in with them, and watch an episode of *Brooklyn 99*, Dad's second-favorite show, instead of being stuck with traitors and alleged club members.

"Hey, this milkshake's fantastic," Gia said.

"Sshh . . ." Rushad nudged her.

"What? I think it's from Savi's plant," Gia responded. "Isn't it?"

I wanted to nod, but I felt fully frozen.

"Let us explain," Sana said.

"But wait . . . first . . ."

"Are you okay?" asked Rushad.

"Like really, really okay?" Gia translated as the wasp buzzed up and promptly settled back onto her collar. "Wasp is asking, so basically Tree is asking, and so you have to answer, you know."

"We wanted to come sooner."

"But Samar said to give you some time."

"Oye!" Samar said, throwing up his arms.

"Don't 'oye' us! We'd have been here the same moment if you hadn't told us to back off."

I was going to snap at them and say of course I was okay, but suddenly I was overcome with a strange feeling. I realized I felt safe, like I did with Tree, that I was among friends. People who actually cared, who were here to check on me, who didn't abandon me now that the so-called work was done. And friends who shared losses.

"Plus, we brought pie!" Samar said, holding up a box and opening it. A shiny globule of banoffee pie was pasted to the corner of the box. "Well, a fair amount of pie, at least. I may have squashed it as we came—too many potholes in this city."

"Hand it over," I said, with a grin.

"She smiles," Gia said. "Wow!"

I began laughing. "Okay, explain now," I said, taking the box from Samar and digging into the banoffee pie, which turned out to be excellent. Dad would have totally loved it. For the first time in ages, I realized I was thinking about my father without my heart twisting into itself. I felt a pang, but this was nice too—to remember him, happily.

Everyone started speaking at once, until Samar finally said, "Folx, folx, may I? I feel I owe Savi an explanation the mostest."

Everyone fell silent. Including Samar.

"Really, Samar, now would be a good time," Sana said, shaking her head exasperatedly after a few minutes. Rushad was chipping at his thumbnail which was painted yellow this time.

"Talking, talking," Samar said, putting his hands up. "Well . . . first we're so relieved you're all right. Well, as all right as can be, given you were just ambushed and almost kidnapped by a . . ."

"Plague of pigeons?" I finished for him.

Everyone burst out laughing again.

"Right," Samar said. "Who knew they were pigeons, dude? That was so surreal."

"I know, right," I replied. "I almost fainted in shock."

"Or in revulsion."

"Or just, you know, plain hilarity."

"Or absurdness."

Gia cleared her throat. "Samar, Savi . . ."

I sat back on the sofa and grinned as Bekku jumped on my lap. I patted her, forgiving her traitorous cuddles with Samar. "Go on."

Samar, in fits and starts, with the help of the Eco Ents, pizza, mulberry milkshake, and banoffee pie, began to explain.

Chapter 34

The Explanation
That Explained

"Turns out TLEU (ATA) have nieces and nephews," Samar said.

"Wizard," I said, holding on to Bekku so I didn't slow-clap his genius. "I figured that out too when they said that the uncles were asking for the status. I was there, remember?"

"No, wait," Rushad said. "We didn't know. We suspected that TLEU (ATA) had to have their own spies in the school. After all, that's where Tree lives. We just didn't know who it was at first. But then we realized that it must be . . ."

"The Very Cool and Hip People," I said.

"Is that what you called them?" Rushad asked.

"Well, in my head," I shrugged. "But then there were so many of them! All across the school."

"Yes, but see, they suddenly became extra-friendly with me," Samar said. "We kind of figured something was up because until then, they weren't giving any Ents any *bhaav*. I mean, they always thought I was uber cool and, you know, fitted their flock." He saw my face and hastily added, "But I kept them at a distance. Anyway, so the Eco Ents made me befriend them." He glared at his friends. "This is all their fault, you know, they made me! Be angry with them, Savi. Not me!"

"Yes, we made you," Gia said, rolling her eyes. "Bro, no one can make you do anything. They knew you were totally hip and cool and," she coughed, "rich—just like them. So next thing we knew, you were accepted into their plague, I mean, fold."

"Aha, so *Alex Rider* of you," I said. Wait, was he a double agent ever? I wasn't sure.

"Listen, it was awful. I should be given a cookie for sacrificing so many hours in their exalted, overbearing company," Samar said, shaking his head frantically. "It was really tiresome. I have never had so many salted rosemary lattes in my life as I did while hanging out with them."

"Oh, and chocolate hazelnut cruffins."

"That too," Samar grinned. "But those I liked. The coffee just gave me acidity." He flushed, feeling like he had given away some big secret. "Anyway . . . so here I was, being like a double agent, transmitting information from one group to the other and back, and it was so hard keeping it all straight at times in my head. I was scared to note it down, because what if someone was hacking my phone?"

"Ever heard of a notebook?" asked Sana, slurping down the last of her milkshake noisily. Clearly, the Ents were losing all sense of boundaries, though that was not surprising after what we had been through.

"Pssh," Samar replied. "Anyway," he said again. "And then you arrived and . . ."

"And Raina realized that Tree was reaching out to me!" I suddenly put two and two together to make twenty-two. "The fig, when it rolled to me, and later the wasp, the Very Cool and Hip People were right there as you ate cold noodles."

Samar winced.

I felt instantly terrible. I knew from Tree that Samar's house was all fragmented since his kid brother had died, and he used to make mock noodles with him, and yet I kept bringing those noodles up again and again.

"Sorry, I didn't mean it that way."

"No offense taken," Samar said. "But I do really like them, you know. You should try them sometime.

Coagulated processed noodles and the steam turning them into mush."

"Gross," yelled Rushad, throwing a cushion at him.

But I wasn't listening to them. It now made sense why Raina, Badal, and all had gone out of their way to befriend me after being so mean to me at first. They had seen that Tree and I shared a special relationship.

I laughed. A year ago, if someone had told me that a ficus tree and I would have a special relationship, I would have kicked their behinds to the moon and back. And now, Tree was perhaps one of the beings that mattered to me the most in the world.

As if she knew what I was thinking, Bekku let out a plaintive meow. "Right with you, Bekku," I whispered. "Only the fate of this city doesn't sit on your shoulders." I patted her and nodded. "Why didn't you tell me all this?"

"*Yaar*, you were already jumpy about magic and cults and tree hugging, how could we tell you about villainous nieces and nephews?" Rushad pointed out. "So Samar was instructed to keep an eye on you."

"Fat lot of good I did," Samar said, looking upset. He ran his hands through his hair, making it stand even more on edge than usual, and then covered his face with his hands. "I think they suspected something was up with me, and they didn't tell me anything. They just asked me to show up at school that night. I can't believe I let that happen, Savi. I am so, so sorry. Really, I was so scared, and you were so brave, and I didn't quite know what to do."

"Especially when they turned into pigeons," I added unhelpfully.

"That too!" Samar looked up, his face all red. "This is all on me. Please, really." He looked so small and woebegone.

"Really, enough," I said, holding up a hand to get him to stop talking. "I admit I was angry with you, with all of you, for keeping the truth from me. But dude, then the wasps showed up, and you were right there calling them—it's all good."

Samar looked a bit relieved. "I wasn't sure if they'd listen to me. They only talk to Gia and for this horrible second, I thought they weren't going to show up. But I guess my skills came in handy."

"I think the pipistrelle told the wasps," Gia said grumpily.

"At least Samar didn't turn into a pigeon," I pointed out. "That would have been unforgivable."

Everyone burst out laughing.

"I don't get it, though," I finally said. "Where are they now? Did they die? Shit, did we kill them?" I stared at Gia's collar, hoping for some answers.

Sana shook her head slowly. "So, it's strange but now there is no sign of them. Like no trace at all. In the school records even. It's like they never existed."

"But three of them were the children of famous people."

"Well, it turns out those actors and politicians have dogs named Mausam and Badal and a Persian cat called Toffee," Gia said. "Even if you scroll way, way down their Insta feeds, it's only these toy dogs." Her voice dropped into a whisper. "Badal the Shih Tzu has hair exactly like, you know, Badal. Of Raina, though, there's no sign."

I was horrified. "You mean they turned into pets? First pigeons, now dogs and cat. I mean dogs and cats are great, but really?" Mom was going to be so upset for her favorite actor.

"Oh no!" Sana said. "Dogs and cats are too good for them. I think it's that reality altered just a bit. I don't know, none of us really do. But let's just say, the natural order of things took over. Everything ultimately goes back to nature."

"Like stardust," Samar said, with a small, sad smile. "And soil."

"Or poop," Gia said. "Nothing goes to waste in nature as well. That would have been fun, if they had turned into dung beetle chow." She sighed as everyone sniggered.

"No thanks, did not want to be showered with poop," Samar said.

"And what about TLEU (ATA)?" I finally asked the one question that had been haunting me.

"They're still going to cut Tree," Rushad said glumly. "It's only been delayed."

WHAT! I felt like I had just been given the best treat in the world and then it had been abruptly snatched away. "You mean all that work was for nothing? The magic, the remembering of the people, the protection spells, the pigeon nieces and nephews exploding into feathers? How!"

"Tree's asked for an emergency meeting," Sana said, looking down at her shoes. "Tree will only talk when all of us are there. Maharukh Sir, Amba Ma'am, and Push-paji are waiting for us."

I immediately made to get up, and Bekku yowled. "What are we waiting for? Let's go then," I said urgently.

Gia picked up a last slice of cold pizza and looked at it miserably as she wrapped it up in tissue paper. "*Chalo*, let's go," she said with a voice that conveyed the exact opposite.

Chapter 35

This Will Not Be Goodbye

"Give me a second!" I dashed into my room and plucked a jasmine flower from our plant.

"Wish me luck, Dad," I whispered.

I hollered a "I'll be right back" to Mom and Meher (while thinking they really did give me too much freedom, letting me step out yet again without asking too many questions—the last time I had almost died. Or at least had almost been turned into a pigeon poop–fossilized statue).

Gia was holding out her hand. I hesitated first and then took it. Fine, the perils of having friends—they hugged you and sometimes held your hand. I could live with that.

A number of autorickshaws and car rides later, we reached our samosa school.

"I cannot believe how many times we've come to

school voluntarily," Sana said with a dramatic sigh. "So disappointing we are, eco-nerd-fighters."

Pushpaji was at the gate and she put her hand on my head, making me feel like a little child again. I smiled at her, and she said, "We're here na, with you, *hamesha*. Come now."

"Your son?" I stammered.

"They lied, and I came rushing back the moment I realized." Pushpaji looked stricken. I wanted to hug her, and so, predictably, I did.

Honestly, I thought I would be terrified of going back to school after what had happened. Memories of that night came slashing back, but I steadied myself. I was surrounded by friends, and in some ways it felt like having another family of sorts. Like when I was with Dad. It was a different feeling, but it felt good.

Amba Ma'am wheeled in from behind us. "How much time you all took! Must have been Samar only, always late." She stretched her arms and recited, "'I wasted time, and now doth time waste me; For now hath—'"

"'—time made me his numbering clock: My thoughts are minutes; and with sighs they jar,'" Samar finished with a grin. A tiny black and red beetle came and sat on his arm. He peered closely at it and said softly, "It wasn't me this time. It was Savi!"

"WHAT! No, it was Gia and that last slice of pizza," I retorted. Everyone started laughing and turned towards Tree. The laughter died in our throats. Maharukh Sir was sitting by the roots, staring at Tree.

No, no, no, this wasn't happening. Tree had aged in the last few days, withering and weakening. Their branches were bare, they stooped slightly, their roots were weary, brittle. I could feel their power ebbing.

I ran. I couldn't bear it. I ran and ran until I reached Tree and put a shaking hand on the trunk. I pulled my hand back, it was like I had been scorched. I started trembling again as Maharukh Sir said quietly, "They are dying."

The Eco Ents who stood rooted to their spots erupted into speech and action.

"There has to be something we can do."

"What rubbish! They are so not dying—not on my watch, not them too."

"*Yaar*, Tree."

"Wasps, talk to us."

"How can they be, but they were just fine, we did everything."

"It's not too late, we can, you know . . ."

The purple frog croaked on my heart—it was back, heavy, clammy, and bitter. I shook my head. "There's nothing we can do—Sir's right."

Gia was frantically talking to the wasp, who turned and flew back into Tree. "The wasps, they are not saying anything. They have gone quiet." Gia, who never cried, broke down as Sana came and put an arm around her.

"This is all my fault," Samar said. "They are dying because of that night. It was that last act, it was too much for Tree."

As we all felt yet another irreversible loss coming, a grief with feathers, I strangely felt a sense of calm descend on me. I sensed that Maharukh Sir felt the same. I touched a root with my foot. I knew what I had to do. I looked at Sir, and he nodded, white-lipped but resolute.

"Come, triangle," I said. I held out my hands and everyone fell into their places around Tree. I could feel my heartbeat in my ear, drumming hard. My blood rushing in my veins even as Tree's heartwood was collapsing, their life force draining.

The familiar action of standing around Tree seemed to give everyone strength. We grasped each other's hands tightly, as if without that contact, we'd all crumble. At least we had each other.

I held Amba Ma'am's hand on my right and pressed my left one to Tree.

"Tree's old. They want us to let them go."

Rushad let out a sob as Amba Ma'am's face blanched.

Samar's cheeks were streaked with tears and his hands were tight fists. Sana was staring at Tree, as if trying to take them in and tattoo their image in her mind. Gia was shaking her head, and Maharukh Sir had his eyes shut, blocking out the pain, while Pushpaji was staring calmly, sadly at our beloved Tree.

Samar looked like he was going to talk again but I shook my head and said, "Tree gave us everything that night, but not just that night. For thousands of years, Tree and other trees have given and given. We've just taken. It gets tiring, propping up the world on your roots and canopies. We do what we can and then it's time to go. To become soil again. To feed the fungi that were your voice and ears for so long. To become nourishment for the earthworms, to replenish the soil, so that new life grows again."

My breath caught in my throat. I coughed. Amba Ma'am squeezed my right hand. Our wasps rose and buzzed.

"Tree wants us all to put our left hands on their trunk," Gia said—her wasps were talking to her again. As she said that, a branch rustled. The hornbill had returned—one last time.

"I am not saying goodbye," Samar yelled. Seeing the hornbill was the last straw for him. He broke away from the triangle and started backing away. "NOT AGAIN. THIS IS SO UNFAIR."

Chapter 36
A Soft Landing

Samar stopped as he backed into a soft stomach.

We all turned to see a huge group of uncles and two aunties standing behind us. We had been staring so intently at Tree that we had failed to notice them at all. For a second, Samar looked like he had landed into an alternative reality, one where he was part of a laughing club, because all them were laughing maniacally.

He turned again and looked at us. But I suspect we all looked as confused as he felt.

Shoots and roots, I thought, as I realized that we were finally face to face with—

"The League of Extraordinary Uncles," Uncle no. 54 said quite unnecessarily.

"And Two Aunties," Aunty no. 2 added hurriedly, not wanting to be left out of this all-important introduction.

An oily smile stretched on each of the uncles' and aunties' faces. I realized with a jolt that there were so many uncles and aunties we knew—Kulkarni Uncle, Damodar Uncle, Das Uncle, Past Food Nation Uncle, BrakeFast Xpress Uncle, Canteen Uncle, the producers of all those shows, bureaucrats, corporate consultants, and political cogs. Worse, they looked just like their nieces and nephews, malevolent and evil—only less cool and hip.

Maybe that's what my former friends would have looked like many years on. Well, if they had been human. Strangely, I realized their memories were fast fading from my brain. But for now, we had to contend with their uncles and aunties. Wait a minute, were they the same people who had . . . No, they couldn't be.

Maharukh Sir and Amba Ma'am came and stood in front of Samar as if to protect him and their other students. But they needn't have bothered.

"You all seem like happy-looking children who have a bright, wonderful future ahead of them," Uncle no. 54 said. "So nice to see. Think of your future, *betas*."

"You cannot stand in the way of Progress," Uncle no. 78 said, his belly jiggling as he laughed.

"Progress is so important for nation-building," Aunty no. 1 said.

"For world building," Uncle no. 56 said. "As in, the world economy building, not those silly world-building games you play."

"The tree," Uncle no. 54 said loudly, "is finally dying. We didn't even need to bring in our saws. It took one look at us and gave up. So nice to see." I guessed he was talking loudly for Tree to hear.

TLEU (ATA) started to laugh, a cheer that rose and rose like an eerie, wailing wind that gave us goosebumps.

Gia and Rushad strode in front, to argue. But I called out, "Don't you get it? This was never a fight."

The laughter stopped, as if cut by a pair of sharp scissors.

"There is never a fight between nature and progress," Sana said, adding on to what I was saying. "Because without nature, there is no progress."

"What will you eat, breathe, drink?" asked Gia, her gravelly voice ringing across the ground. "Money? It tastes rubbish. And you need trees to even print money."

"Environment and Development have always been two sides of one coin—you chose to see them as a coin toss but without the other side, neither is valuable," Rushad said. He looked angrily at the older men and women in front of them. "You are supposed to be wise— we're meant to look up to you."

TLEU (ATA) looked at each other shiftily. "You children are giving us *gyaan*. You clearly have anger management issues—you should get some help," Uncle no. 45 said, shaking his hair out of his eyes.

I burst out laughing at that. "We're forced to be angry because so many of your generation othered nature. Turning it into a relic, a thing of the past, into something less."

"Into something to be forgotten," Samar said. He waved his hand. "To make it vanish from our memories. So no, you failed at that. We will never forget this. We will never forget Tree."

That's when the images shifted in my mind, like a camera lens coming into focus, and I realized who they were. Though they were now grown up, some of them were the bullies from my dad's childhood. Still bulldozing their way into our future. I wanted do something, but I didn't know what.

As if reading my thoughts, a swarm of wasps broke away from Tree. It was their last defense. They flew towards TLEU (ATA), buzzing angrily, threateningly, once again forming a majestic serpent eagle.

Hurriedly, TLEU (ATA) stared at their phones and smartwatches and exclaimed,

"Oh I have a meeting."

"Already late."

"Car's here."

"The Mrs. has got *hafoos* off season."

"I had forgotten we had that thing."

"Medical test."

And without a second look at the Eco Ents or Tree, they began to walk away.

All except Uncle no. 34.

TLEU (ATA) stopped and looked at him. "Don't you have that thing?" asked Uncle no. 23 helpfully.

Uncle no. 34 shook his head. "I'm done—with the lies, with the distractions. I do have a thing—and it's here, with our future."

Uncle no. 54 gave him a look of disgust, and he looked like he was going to say something but thought better of it. Without another word, TLEU (ATA) melted away.

Uncle no. 34 turned to us and said, "Humblest apologies. May I?"

Maharukh Sir and Amba Ma'am were shaking their heads, but Sana said, "Of course, Uncle. Join us."

Everyone except Samar walked towards Tree. He was rooted there. I made to go get him but then, the wasps gently flew towards Samar, surrounding him as if he was inside a tent.

Then it was almost like the wasps were bearing him back to Tree. I looked at him, and he nodded, as he took his place back in the triangle. The triangle expanded and made way for Uncle.

"Wait, wait for me!" Aunty no. 2 was striding towards us. "They are so boring, ya—same old nonsense. I swear, I am turning over into a new leaf." She giggled, clearly at her own joke. Rushad nodded tightly. Once again, the triangle expanded and made way for Aunty.

A lone wasp broke away and buzzed in front of Gia. We all turned to her, waiting for her to translate, but she shook her head. Not now, she seemed to say. She held out her hand, the wasp sat on it, as if kissing her hand, and the swarm went back to their Tree. Our Tree. I dug into my pocket and removed the jasmine flower, now crumpled and a little brown at the edges. I took a deep breath and buried it in the soil of which Tree was intrinsically a part.

"Here now, rest.
Our grand ficus Tree
Who says you won't walk this earth?
The wind will bear your stories far and away.
Your leafy branches, one with the sky
Your roots, part of the dark underland.
You will stand, stately tall,

Slightly stooped to the wind.
That's how you will remain
In our memory.
Of the cosmos, and of this earth."

We all moved forward and placed our trembling hands on to the trunk. The same green light enveloped our grove of teenagers and adults.

And then, like the darkest of nights that swallows the moon, the light dimmed. Forever.

With a last sigh, a shiver of their branches, Tree died, their heartwood finally giving way.

But as they died, they released their magic. Into the air. Some into us, holding on to Tree for as long as we could. Some into the adults, just a bit. Most into the roots, as it traveled to all the other trees and plants and mangroves, the fungi furiously passing it on from root to root, the magic coursing through their sap and heartwood.

The birds, the wasps, the insects, they were all soaked in a wave of magic.

And then Tree was gone. But not really. They were now of the beetles, the moss, and the birds who would make homes in their hollows. And like memory, like stories, their magic lingered. In each one of us.

Forever.

Epilogue

Two Birthdays

I sat cross-legged on the window ledge in my room. It was like a rainforest in here, with plants spilling from each corner. Well, I had never seen a rainforest, but this is exactly how I imagined it to be. I hugged Bekku tightly until she yowled in protest and wriggled free, heading back to her favorite jasmine plant. Our favorite jasmine plant. It was thriving. All of them were, at least the ones that hadn't died. They swayed in the wind. Every time I reached out to touch one, a bittersweet memory wafted up. But I didn't mind.

Memories were what I had, and they kept Dad alive for me. And it was not just Dad, it was also Tree. Some of the memories were a blur, some sharp, most in-between. But they were a part of me, like Dad and Tree.

Dad's plants—well, our plants—had drastically

reduced in number. Finally, I had let them go into the composter, to become mulch, to replenish the other plants. Where the erstwhile installation of definitely dead plants stood, I had planted seeds gifted to me by the Ents—chili, tomato, *baingan,* and many more. Small shoots were finally poking out of the dark soil.

As they grew, the purple frog around my heart felt less heavy. I know I was much more bearable—in fact, I was even known to smile and laugh with the Ents, though I did tend to snap at Samar a lot, especially when he shoved me in front of his beloved squirmy earthworms. Not that he minded. He just gave me some more trivia about grief and anger and denial. In return, I would roll my eyes at him. He'd then slather on more trivia. Not that I minded.

Outside, a pigeon cooed, and I froze. I still had nightmares involving pigeons and uncles and aunties.

I took a deep breath. The climate hadn't become better, but it had not gotten worse. A hefty price Shajarpurians had paid. But now at least the trees were thriving. On some days it still felt like the city that Dad had grown up in, with crisp air and pure water, but (mostly) nicer people.

Even though . . .

I turned and looked at my desk and bookcase. There was the family photo of Dad gardening and right next to it, a photo of me, pressing my left hand to Tree's trunk. It never stops hurting, I realized, as sadness washed over me afresh, like a wave crashing onto the shore. It just finds new ways of being—some days it stung more, and some days it curled up into the feathered thing called grief.

TLEU (AOA)'s stronghold had lessened on the city as they found more and more citizens falling in love with nature—heads over heels, proper, filmy love. A song and dance kind of eternal love.

But they, the TLEU (AOA), didn't just vanish. Ha! Wishes were not horses. The group was too big and powerful and conniving. Oh so many words to describe them. Amba Ma'am would have a field day with that. They were everywhere, and yet, this had been a big blow for them. A first for them. Or so our Uncle and Aunty khabri told us. Every time I thought of TLEU (AOA) standing there, sneering at us and Tree, I felt so angry. I wanted to yell, or do something. Worst, they were already regrouping, conspiring, throwing dance parties, building statues, and moving on to the next tree. But, so were we, the Ents. At least, our school had got collective amnesia over the need for an Olympic-sized swimming pool in the backyard, and was instead living up to its name. Mrs. Pankhida, it was rumored, had been spotted among the dancers around the trees.

TLEU (AOA) kept trying new things, new projects, their threat far from over. But now the people remembered. With the force of those memories, many rallied together for nature, for their future, and kept the meddling league at bay. The magic of Tree had also sealed the city against more destruction. But TLEU (AOA) continued to spread their Distraction, Destruction everywhere else. Across the country, internationally. So we were constantly on alert, swapping news with other eco clubs across the world. Well, most of the Ents were, at least. I was still hibernating. However, it helped that Uncle no. 34 and Aunty no. 2 were on our side, feeding us bits of information. They also brought lots of snacks, and so, slowly, we had forgiven them. Kind of.

Bekku padded up to me and jumped onto my lap again. "Do you know why Dad named me Savitri?" I asked Bekku, who clearly didn't care, as long as the gibberish-talking human kept her well-fed.

"He named me after his hero, Savitribai Phule. She was so brave, so very cool—a pioneer in girls' education. She did so many things, including starting the first school for girls of all castes. You know, I wouldn't be studying perhaps if she hadn't taken that first bold step. Even though the upper castes tried to break her spirit. I *LOVE* it."

Bekku meowed in response.

"When Tree was dying, they shared more of his memories with me." I closed my eyes, transported back to that moment. "And then . . . the wasps told Gia that Dad would be so proud of me. That I was living up to the name that he had chosen for me." I let out a sob. Immediately, Bekku moved closer and started purring and kneading my lap with her paws.

I started crying, sobs racking my body. It was a secret that I had kept to myself, deliciously close, bringing it out only when I needed it—like today. It was Dad's birthday—a day that used to be special, a day of ice cream cake and parties, of dinners at fun restaurants, of cook-a-thons at home, and weeks of planning presents and quizzes.

What a year and a half it had been. And we had survived it. Kind of.

Meher (now at 11,002 followers and counting), Mom (no longer a Damien-type cleaning human), and me (a slightly more bearable person) had decided to mark his birthday by creating a new tradition. We would plant a tree in Dad's name every year. And of course, there would be cake. Duh.

The only thing, there was one big problem.

Mom had threatened to bake a tres leches cake,

another favorite of Dad's. Meher and I had invented an emergency shopping trip to distract her. I giggled, distractions did work sometimes for the greater good. Like that of our stomachs.

Look at me, crying one minute and laughing the next. I moved Bekku gently and got up to wash my face.

Just then, my phone pinged. It was the Eco Ents. We had a club meeting today. I had skipped because of Dad's birthday. They had offered to come over, but I wanted to be alone with my family. And anyway, I'd see them tomorrow before we left for Almora to spend the Christmas vacation with Baba.

I slid open the phone and my heart danced a little. It was a video—Samar, Sana, Rushad, Gia, Amba Ma'am, and Maharukh Sir were right where Tree lived. A pair of parakeets peeked out of a small hollow. A third tiny gray-green head popped out from the hole. Lichen and fungi lovingly embraced our grand old Tree. Always the Mother Tree, even after their death. A wasp was perched on Gia's collarbone, while, yikes, a pipistrelle poked out of Samar's pocket, its brown nose just visible. Pushpaji had gone back to her village to be with her son, taking over their family farm, where she was going to let the wild trees take over and practice organic farming. We had promised to visit her soon.

Right by Tree, a small green shoot poked out of the ground.

I looked closely—at the edge of Gia's left ear, another wasp hovered. In the distance, I saw the hornbill fly from Tree to the silk cotton tree. I smiled through my tears.

The message on the group read: "They are back, Savitree!"

Acknowledgments

When I first found out about the Wood Wide Web, I immediately wanted to visit the understories of trees to hear, see, feel those stories they share. I spent months reading books and articles and listening to podcasts by Robert Macfarlane, Greta Thunberg, Robin Wall Kimmerer, Harini Nagendra and Seema Mundoli, Ranjit Lal, Mike Shanahan, Peter Wohlleben; taking walks with Karthikeyan Srinivasan, Radha Rangarajan; then I read scientist Suzanne Simard's work who, like Rushad, is my hero. I discovered—trees communicate with each other, travel, share nutrients, and even send distress signals. Basically, they are awesome.

From that science, mixed with the magic and wonder that's nature, came Tree and Savi's story, and the understory of grief. This book's roots are intertwined in earthworm-holes and stardust that's Abhiyan Humane, who now conveniently won't read anything I write. Fine, I will talk to my zombie aloe vera and definitely dead rosemary. But well, this book's for you.

Sending thank you signals to my book's mycorrhizal network—

Agent K aka Kanishka Gupta, who believed in this book.

Daniel Ehrenhaft for being the warmest and coolest editor, who like a seedpod planted Savi's story in new lands.

Rajiv Eipe for the wasps and walks and for this gorgeous cover.

Gayle Forman, Gail Lerner, and Mathangi Subramanian for reading and loving Savi and Tree's story, and welcoming it to the US. Jairam Ramesh, Jerry Pinto, and Prerna Singh Bindra for their kind words on reading the book.

Team Blackstone, especially Kelley Lusk, Joe Garcia, Brendan Deneen, Isabella Nugent, Francie Crawford, Rebecca Malzahn, and Josh Stanton for being truly amazing.

Deepanjana Pal, who is my personal Atwood. Aparna Kapur, excellent opinion generator, sentence finisher, and mind reader. Shinibali Mitra Saigal, who is always in my corner. Ravikant Kisana, for all the heartwood-warming stuff.

Nimmy Chacko, dragon editor, who is supportive, sharp, and as awesome as trees. Vatsala Kaul Banerjee and Team Hachette for their tireless work with the book in India. Radha Rangarajan and Vena Kapoor for the much-needed stern fact checking.

Sudeshna Shome Ghosh, Lavanya Karthik, Shals Mahajan, Rohit Kulkarni, Sangeeta Bhansali, LOW Lives, Aastha Chauhan, Aditya Narula, Suzanne Singh, Sayoni Basu, and Ruchira Gupta for the cheerleading.

Prerna, Prashant Rao, Rohan Chakravarty, fellow earthworm-hole finders. And each one of you, who reached out to me over emails, meetings, social media to share your grief.

My families—the Vachharajanis and Humanes. Anoop Kumar and Team Nalanda.

Shajarpur is fictional because in today's climate-changed world, I couldn't situate a city with perfect climate, as it does not exist. But mother trees like Tree do. As long as we have these wonders, our heartwood can hope for a better climate future.